HOT-BLOODED BRIBE

"Well, we meet again, Deacon."

Eli whipped around to look into the provocative sea-green eyes of Marilee Weatherby. She was wearing a tight blouse that made a major production out of her full, lush breasts and the narrow perfection of her waist.

"Be advised, Eli Holten, Chief Scout of the Twelfth Calvalry," she said softly, batting her long lashes, "I saw you rescue that poor wounded officer. One word from me could bring you instant death. But don't worry, I won't tell. Provided—"

She paused and licked tempting red lips with a moist pink tongue.

"Provided what?"

"Only that you show me some friendly attention. I . . . a girl gets lonely. I'm sure you understand what I mean?"

Eli felt his pulse quicken and tasted a familiar tanginess.

"As a matter of fact I'm a bit ahead of you," he told her.

He swung Marilee off her f⸻ d her squealing up the rungs of ⸻t. He set her free and it ⸻ r her to remove her ri⸻

"Come to ⸻w."

With such ⸻ion, the scout could not refuse. . . .

#17
THE SCOUT

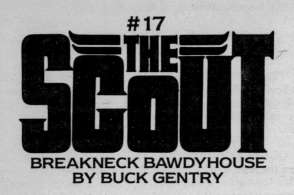

BREAKNECK BAWDYHOUSE
BY BUCK GENTRY

ZEBRA BOOKS
KENSINGTON PUBLISHING CORP.

Special acknowledgements to Mark K. Roberts

ZEBRA BOOKS

are published by

Kensington Publishing Corp.
475 Park Avenue South
New York, NY 10016

First printing: January 1985

Printed in the United States of America

This Book is dedicated, with respect, to a great writer and a good friend, *ROBERT SKIMMIN*.

B.G.

"*Keen of eye, sharp of ear, with bold, confident demeanor, the civilian scouts who guided our military forces into the teeth of hostile action remain godlike in proportion to those of us who had to rely upon their knowledge . . .*"

—General Granville Martin
U.S. Infantry, Indian
Campaigns

"*A scout — to be good — had to have a foot in both camps.*"

—Pike Kimberly, Scout
U.S. Cavalry

Chapter 1

Tall, straight pines concealed from view seventy heavily armed Sans Arc Sioux braves, painted for war and mounted on their finest warponies. Kicking Elk, their leader, sat astride his snorting stallion in the place of honor at the center of the long, slightly in-curved line of fighting men. Intelligence crackled from his obsidian eyes as he glanced left and right.

Satisfied with his survey of the warparty, he gave a nod of assent. His hawk-beak of a nose cleaved the air like the prow of a ship through the waves. Red, yellow, and green lines of warpaint formed lightning bolt patterns on both of his bronze cheeks, and a black circle turned his mouth into the gaping maw of doom. He was privileged to wear the thirty-eight-eagle-feather bonnet of a highly successful and respected war chief. Its long train of feathers and beaded elkhide drape had been tied into place up his back, so that he had the aspect of a proud and virile turkey cock. The straight slash of high cheekbones divided his face horizontally, giving an aura of formidable strength to his austere features. Slowly he brought his eyes to focus on the long, downhill run to the small settlement in a bowl-like valley of the Black Hills.

"Wašicun!" He spat the word like profanity.

The white men had come, his thoughts continued. This sacred place had been profaned. The *hèsapa* had been granted to the Dakota for all times under the treaty Red Cloud had signed.

But what did that mean to the *wašicun*? They made treaties only to break them. Worse, they had come *here*.

"They must be destroyed," he had argued in council. "For these new whites have chosen to build a village of lust and liquor on the very ground where the Spirit has shown me in a dream that we are to hold the Sun Dance. Now is the time, and that is the place appointed by the Great Spirit. We must cleanse the ground! I have spoken."

No voice rose in dispute. Old gray heads nodded sagely, and the younger men yipped and slapped their bare thighs in agreement. And so it had happened. The Sans Arc had left their lodges along the Yellowstone and ridden eastward into the holy Black Hills. What they found was as it had been foretold by messengers and scouts.

Whites had built six wooden lodges in the Valley-Where-the-Sky-Fell. In the center of this arrangement stood a great mystery. A tall lodge made of red stones, each exactly like the others. For three days, Kicking Elk scouted the tightly enclosed, grassy bowl. He sent others, and they shared their impressions of what they saw. It could be done. Not more than three times two hands of *wašicun* men inhabited the place. All of the others were women. It awaited only his signal and the seventy Sans Arc warriors would fall on the whites like hungry wolves on an orphaned fawn.

"Hu ihpeya wicayapo!" Kicking Elk screeched as he

raised his feathered warlance.

"*Huka hey!*" the warriors echoed.

Then, each howling his individual warcry, the Sans Arc swept down upon the unsuspecting village.

It was indeed a good day to die.

Inside the town of Breakneck Gap, a bell began to ring stridently as the wailing Sioux raced over the grassy slope toward the buildings nestled in the bottom of the vast depression. A moment later, incongruous as it seemed, a boatswain's pipe sounded.

"All hands man the barricades!" a British-accented voice bawled. "Stand by to repel boarders. Gunners to the magazine!"

Capt. William C. Weatherby slipped into the heavy blue brocaded coat with the well-worn lace trim, gold buttons, and floorbrush epaulettes of gold braid which he had worn every day of his life since receiving his first command in the Royal Navy. He adjusted a cocked hat on his head and raised his arms, while his striker buckled his sword belt in place. With a final flick of long, aesthetic fingers on his tight, white trousers, to remove a random fleck of cigar ash, Captain Weatherby stepped out into the street and strode calmly to the western end of town, from where he could hear the howls of his enemy and see their rumbling approach.

Careful to keep his face impassive, he studied the swarming savages. He noted their seemingly invincible numbers and took stock of his own defenses. Some twenty men stood ready on this side, weapons in hand. Hardly a sufficient force, the former sea captain considered.

11

Yet all were disciplined and drilled — capable fighting men. They should be able to hold off the savages long enough. A young boy of thirteen, who'd have been a midshipman had they been at sea, ran up and saluted smartly.

"Mr. Yardley's compliments, sir. They're ready to run out the guns."

"Thank you, Mr. Tandy. Have Mr. Yardley stand by. I think we'll test their mettle a bit first."

"Aye-aye, Captain."

The Sioux, by then, had come within rifle range. Those possessing such weapons opened up in a ragged line of fire. Bullets whined and moaned through town, most of them aimed high. A window broke in the bordello at Weatherby's back. He noted the shrieks from inside and the tinkle of falling glass and stepped further into the open, a brass telescope to one eye.

"Hummm," he remarked to no one in particular. " 'Pears to be about seventy of the buggers. Well, lads," he spoke up. "Give 'em what all, eh?"

Under the calm commands of petty officers, a thunderous volley ripped into the ranks of the charging Sans Arcs. Its deadly accurate aim broke off the attack, and the warriors wheeled and rode away, yipping, to gather for another assault.

"Look at 'em run!" one youthful defender shouted.

In his exuberance, he stood up too soon, only to sit down rapidly, a look of wonder on his face as he examined the red-and-green painted arrow that decorated his chest. His spirit quickly joined those of five dead Indians who lay beyond the hastily erected barricades that blocked off access to Breakneck Gap.

With a whoop of defiance, Kicking Elk turned his

warriors and led the second attack against the determined whites.

This time the charging Sioux reached the barrier of dirt-laden wagons that blocked the street and surged over them. Stone warclubs flashed in the midday sun, and men began to fall among the defenders. Arrows hummed and hissed through the air. From the second story of another brothel, a moan of despair rose from the mouth of one hapless, unwilling inmate.

Face powder-white, the soiled dove clasped both hands to her cheeks, and her eyes rolled wildly. Down the street, from a sturdy, tower-like brick building, came a rumble as two pieces of artillery rolled out of wide double doors. Behind the brightly shining brass tubes came their caissons. Sweating, barefoot men strained to pull the cumbersome devices toward the area of hottest conflict.

The two sets of carriages and caissons rumbled past the pair of saloons and three bordellos that comprised the remainder of Breakneck Gap, and swung into place near where Captain Weatherby stood. Sensing the moods of the frightened prostitutes, the former naval officer looked up over his shoulder at them. He gave the terrified women a cruel smile and only the slightest of nods to acknowledge their presence. They were making him a fortune, the onetime commanding officer of the *Euripides* gloated. Be that as it may, he decided, he had better get back to the matter at hand.

"Ho, there, Mr. Yardley. Lively now and get those guns into position."

"Aye-aye, Cap'n," a graying, stoop-shouldered man in a uniform coat that identified him as a ship's First Officer replied. "Heave, men. Heave. That's it. Drop those trails now. Good . . . good. Make sure they set well. Gunners, depress to minimum elevation.

"You there, loaders. Bring up the cartridges." Yardley paced back and forth amid a hail of Sioux bullets and arrows, indifferent to the danger around him. "Open breaches!"

"Ready one!"

"Ready two!"

Yardley looked over, expectantly, at Captain Weatherby.

Weatherby raised one hand and held it as Kicking Elk's Sans Arc warriors whirled their frothing-mouthed warponies and swarmed together for another assault.

"There's your target, Mr. Yardley."

A moment later, Weatherby dropped his hand in a rustle of lace trim at the cuff.

The clear, blue sky of Dakota Territory ripped asunder from the roar of two Whitworth Screwbreech Rifles. The twin demons of naval gunnery belched flame and recoiled satisfactorily. Unseen power set their impoverished trails and raised the wheels six inches off the ground. A great billow of smoke obscured the street and, beyond, the howling Sioux.

Canister shot slashed into the charging savages. It indiscriminately tore at horse and human flesh. The heavy musketoon balls gouged out huge hunks of meat and sent blood flying in a crimson mist. Warcries changed to howls of agony and the hideous moans of the dying. Again, Weatherby dropped his hand in signal, and the Whitworth guns fired a second salvo.

Borne by the deadly shot casings, the scythe of the Grim Reaper claimed another dozen braves. Horsehair and hide, bronze skin and eagle feathers filled the air amid a maelstrom of dust and powder smoke. Instantly, Kicking Elk ordered a retreat.

As the surviving warriors streamed away from the invincible town of Breakneck Gap, the Whitworth rifles & cannon kept up a steady thunder. Their range superior to that of conventional muzzle-loading cannon, the powerful guns continued to range on the fleeing Sioux. The vicious canister rounds claimed victims until the last brave disappeared into the narrow gap that afforded the only access to the once serene valley where in ancient times a meteor had crashed to earth. At the center of the bowl formed by the alien visitor, a hearty cheer rose from the defenders.

"Bravo, Father," a sweet voice praised from the balcony of the third bordello.

"Thank you, Marilee, my dear," Captain Weatherby responded. He looked up with a proud and possessive expression at the lovely young woman.

Marilee Weatherby stood poised in a dramatic pose, her lemon-silk-gloved left hand clutching the braided leather handle of a parasol, while the other rested lightly on her right breast. Her trim, wiry figure hid behind the ruffles and gusseting of a high-fashion creation in yellow and white, shipped direct from Paris, France, by order of her doting father. Lovely sea-green eyes reflected great intelligence and hot passions, some as yet untapped. She wet naturally ruby lips with the pink tip of her pliant tongue and affected a winsome smile.

"Such a ruddy lot of blood, though, don't you think, Father?" she inquired, her voice taking a plunge into the coarse gutter accent of a Cockney fishmonger.

"Please, Marilee! One must remain conscious of one's station at all times. How should it look to these men to

15

see their betters conducting themselves like common cocklemongers?"

"Really, Father. This *is* America, you know. Everyone is supposed to be equal here."

"Not in Breakneck Gap, Marilee. Here we preserve all the traditions of the English social order and the regulations of the Royal Navy."

"From which you slunk off into the night in disgrace, don't forget, dear father."

"*Marilee!* We shall take this up later. Now, I must attend to the surgeon and discover our butcher's bill. Mister Yardley, have the men stand down. Boatswain, pipe Up Spirits."

Cheering men left the ramparts to collect the spoils of war, while two burly bartenders from the largest saloon rolled out an oaken barrel of potent Jamaican rum. They breached the cask and began to ladle up one-pint pewter mugs, half-filled with water. As they worked and the gun crews secured the Whitworths, Marilee Weatherby stepped through a pair of French doors and descended the stairs to greet her father as he entered the large reception area of the sporting house. She crossed to him with open arms.

"Forgive my little tweaking of your sore spot, Father," she murmured as she kissed his cheek. "That was a masterful display of superior firepower over vast numbers. You directed the entire battle in a magnificent manner. I'm truly proud of you."

"Thank you, dearest Marilee. Had you but been a son—"

"What difference does that make? I have learned celestial navigation, shiphandling, gunnery and now the tactics of Indian fighting like any midshipman. I am every bit as qualified to take your place eventually as any son. Grant me that, at least, Father."

"I—" Weatherby's heart softened and he took the shapely young woman into his arms. "You win again, Marilee. How can I deny you anything?"

"When can I go to New York, or Paris, or Berlin, then, Father?"

William Weatherby stepped back abruptly. A deep frown line marred his smooth forehead. "No one leaves Breakneck Gap, Marilee. Not the whores, not my seamen, not you nor I. It—It's not safe in the outside world. Here we have a haven in which to build an empire. Don't ever suggest leaving again."

Safely outside the narrow pass that led to the sacred valley, Kicking Elk halted his men to take stock. The results far from pleased him. He had lost too many men. How could he carry on? Where would more warriors come from to destroy this profanation of their most holy of places? He turned to his second in command, Stone Heart.

"We will ride until the sun leaves us. Then we make camp. First, I want to talk to my brothers."

Stone Heart gathered the remaining Sans Arc warriors around their leader and took his usual place to Kicking Elk's immediate left.

"We did not know of the mighty guns that speak at a long distance," the warchief began his oration. "Our numbers are fewer now. We will call upon the men of the Oglala, the *Minikayawoźupi*, the *Witanhantahipi* and even our cousins the *Sahiela*."

"Will the Cheyenne join us?"

17

"It is their sacred ground, too," Kicking Elk answered the doubter. "The *Saheila* will break camp and come. We will ask them to stay for the Sun Dance after the big battle that will purify the Valley-Where-the-Sky-Fell. To make our war one of bigness, we will fight other whites. Raid the mud lodges of those who break apart the soil to the south of here. Attack the mighty horse that runs on iron rails. Then our brothers and cousins will beg to join in our holy enterprise. If many whites must die to rid our land of these evil ones, so be it! I have spoken."

Chapter 2

Capt. William Weatherby strode about his small domain feeling immensely proud of himself. How much he had accomplished in the short time since the American War! His indiscretion aboard the *Euripides* would have sealed his fate, had he chosen to remain and face the consequences. His dealing in contraband *might* have gone on indefinitely without discovery. Yet any probing Admiralty inquiry into why he had happened to be short on powder when the Yankee blockage frigate challenged him would have uncovered all sorts of irregularities.

How humiliating! To have been outgunned by a frigate, which carried only eighteen twelve-pounders to his own complement of forty-two guns of twenty-four and thirty-two-pound caliber. His gunners might as well have tried to throw the roundshot, considering that he had sold, at enormous profit, two-thirds of the powder supply of the *Euripides* to Southern guerrillas, fighting in Texas.

As a result, the rigging and hull of the larger ship had been riddled by American shot, and the decks awash with blood from fiery shell fragments. Rather than submit himself to the indignities of a board of inquiry and eventual courtmartial, he had chosen to let it appear that he had gone down with his ship. Many in his crew had elected to join him. Their greatest *coup* had been to make off with the two shiny-new Whitworth Rifles, which he had obtained from the hold of the American frigate.

Weatherby had struck his colors and then treacherously fired a broadside into the Yankee vessel when it lay alongside. Boarders swarmed over the smaller ship and quickly secured the enemy craft. Packed away in the cargo hold had been the Whitworth guns and nearly a thousand rounds of ammunition. These he saw as a means to escape the awful truths awaiting him upon his return to the Caribbean Station in Jamaica, or later in Portsmouth. It was rare indeed that a captain ever led a mutiny aboard his own ship. William Weatherby did just that.

In order to silence forever any who had knowledge of his deeds, he and those who had participated in the years of illicit traffic engineered the deaths of the officers and men whom the captain felt might turn Queen's evidence against them. Then they sank the *Euripides* and sailed away aboard the frigate. Four years later, he discovered the meteor-formed valley in the Black Hills of Dakota Territory.

Carefully, over the next seven years, he built up a loyal following, purchased supplies and building materials, and laid plans for a sort of haven for those who had no love of the law. Six months earlier, he had finally moved into the valley and founded Breakneck Gap. Now the Sioux had come to dispute his claim. They would not succeed, he could guarantee that. He looked out toward the recent battlefield and saw his men returning.

Several carried blood-smeared pouches of flesh, the scrotums of dead Indians, which they would tan and make into tobacco pouches. All seemed in a festive mood, heightened by generous swallows of the grog served up at his order. He stepped out onto the balcony of the bordello and raised his arms to gain their attention.

"You fought well today, men. The heathen savages have decided to contest our right to be here. I know how you feel about that. And I know what will happen to them if they come back." A huge cheer rose from the thirty powder-grimed residents of Breakneck Gap.

"That's not enough, though. We must carry the fight to the enemy. We will organize raids against the Sioux in reprisal for their affrontery in attacking us here. We will burn their tipis, steal away their women, and kill all the bucks we encounter. You." Weatherby pointed to a tall, lean, grimy man standing closest to the brothel. "Freddy Mullins. I'm placing you in charge of organizing and carrying out these raids. Choose the men you will need, and be prepared to start off first thing tomorrow morning."

"Aye, Cap'n." Mullins scratched at some encrusted dirt behind one ear with a blunt, grubby finger. He pushed his tall fur cap to a rakish angle and swaggered over the open hogshead of rum.

"Fill 'er up, Jake," he instructed the bartender. "You all heard the cap'n, boys. Now which ones of you want a chance at a little fresh, young Injun pussy?"

Funny, he'd never given much thought to the profession of journalism, Eli Holten thought as he lay nude upon the crisp white sheets of the big bed. The chief scout for the Twelfth U.S. Cavalry had always thought of reporters as being gruff-voiced, cigar-smoking, whiskey-swilling men in derby hats. Not so the blonde beauty who hovered over him at that moment.

Thick waves of her heady woman-scent emanated

from the juicy cleft that hung only inches from Eli's face. Firm, full breasts swayed invitingly from her trim chest as she bobbed her head and shoulders up and down. Inordinately talented lips and tongue sent shivers of delight through the rangy, muscular frame of the stalwart scout. He tingled with sheer joy as she inscribed a spiral around the broad, arrow-head tip of his throbbing organ. Then she engulfed it and began to slather him all over.

With one small hand, Rachel Johnson cupped the heavy sack that hung below the thick, long member she serviced and began to knead the contents gently. She was a rarity in being a female newspaper reporter. Rarer still, the scout considered, had been her incredible talent in bed. At his suggestion, he had spent the night with her and quickly discovered that her wide, full hips were firm and resourceful. Her slim waist had been a startling contrast to the flare below and her remarkably large, solid breasts. They had made love twice, swiftly and competently, before Rachel relaxed and began to talk about herself.

"How is it that an Eastern newspaper came to send a woman out to so desolate a place?" Eli had inquired as their banked fires cooled slightly.

"They don't know that I'm a woman," Rachel had responded. "All communications with my editor are written under the name of John Morrison. A, uh, an acquaintance of mine once posed as John Morrison and had lunch with the editor and publisher of the *Boston Herald*. They went away impressed. So," the striking beauty went on as she idly stroked Holten's hard, flat belly and worked her way down to the already rising shaft that poked from a lush patch of curly black hair, "when things got hot out here, the editor decided to send 'John Morrison' to get the real story."

"Which 'real story?'"

"About how the Army handles bandits on the frontier, and what is being done about the terrible savages," Rachel had told him.

Holten had found it all quite amusing. Likewise the swift and passionate manner in which the hungry lass had brought him fully erect and straddled his supine form. Now, with a prodigious slurping gulp, she ingested fully half of the scout's swollen lance and began to massage it with mobile lips. Her powerful perfume overwhelmed Eli, and he reached up to spread wide the sweet-tasting pink lips that masked the wonderfully tight and active passage leading to her central core. His tongue flicked forward to tease the leafy fronds. With fluid expertise, Holten worked his lapping stroke upward until he encountered the large protrusion of her fun node. It was above normal in size, like a small penis, and he curled his sinuous lingual muscle around it in such a manner that it brought forth a murmur of approval from the overjoyed recipient.

"Didn't your mother teach you not to talk with your mouth full?" Eli quipped as he interrupted his delicious ministrations.

Her stifled giggles sent new thrills through his turgid member.

Deftly they worked each other toward a thunderous climax. Only seconds short of her release, Rachel broke off her studied attentions to Holten's iron-hard rod and slid forward until she could impale herself on his pillar of womanly delight.

Slowly she ground her hips in a circular motion as she lunged up and down, taking fully every wonderful bit of the scout's manhood. Eli joined her, extending the totality of his penetration with thrusting pelvis and glorying in the unspeakably marvelous sensations which her agile contractions were sending through his sensitive device. She sensuously sighed her way through one completion, then another, while slowly she built the fires that raged in his loins. And, oh, how she delighted in it.

Rachel had been far from a nervous virgin when she dashed off her clothes and entered the bed with Eli. She had gleefully surrendered her maidenhead some ten years earlier, at the tender age of thirteen, to the awkward and astonished — though handsome — boy who delivered groceries to her family home on Beacon Hill. So anxious had she been to be relieved of the unwanted impediment, Rachel had felt not the slightest pain as the youth, who was barely seven months older than herself, had jerkily inserted his slim, rigid penis. Although both had been virginal at the start of the afternoon's pleasantries, they had invented several delightful distractions before the encounter ended. From that time on, Rachel had never shirked in her quest for greater knowledge and skill.

So by the time she lay in the brawny arms of the sun-browned scout, she had become a veritable encyclopedia of sexual charms and dalliances. His own vast experience had only added piquant savor to the hedonistic broth they set about brewing. In the midst of her happy reflections, Rachel suddenly arched her back and drove herself with renewed energy against Eli's pubic arch.

With a hot gush that left him weak and dizzy, Eli exploded over the edge and emptied his life force into the pulsating recepticle that tightly clinched him. In a fever of delirious spasm, they matched each other eruption for eruption. At last the raging inferno subsided, and they sprawled on the bed in sheer exhaustion.

"You're some man, Eli," Rachel murmured in contentment. "More than most women deserve."

"Yourself excluded?"

"Of course. I have to compete in a man's world every day. When I, uh, let my hair down, naturally I feel I have a right to something special. Right now, you're my 'something special.' "

"That's flattering."

"I meant it to be."

The pleasant glow of their after-love conversation dissolved in the battering of knuckles at the door of Rachel's hotel room. Frowning, Eli called out a challenge.

"Who is it?"

"Sergeant McInnes. I have a message for you from General Corrington, Mister Holten."

Reluctantly, Eli climbed from the bed and slid into trousers. He padded over to the door on bare feet and opened it.

"How the hell did the General know to find me here?" he complained.

McInnes had the puckish face of a leprechaun. When he grinned knowingly, it only added to the illusion. He looked up from his short stature at the tall, broad-shouldered scout and turned on his widest grin.

"He didn't know *exactly* where to find you, sir. The way the general put it was like this. 'Sergeant McInnes,' he says to me, 'go find out where the newest, prettiest and most eligible female is staying, and I think you'll find Holten there.' And that's what I did, sir."

"Give me the damned note and don't be a smart-ass," Holten growled.

After the sergeant stepped out into the hallway to wait

25

as escort, Holten ripped open the folded sheet of heavy linen paper and scanned the lines. Rachel stretched languidly on the bed and studied him with curious gray eyes.

"What is it, Eli dear?"

"The General's compliments, and would I be so kind as to report to his office. Damn! It has to be an assignment. And that grizzled old fart always saves the hard ones for me." He crossed to the bed and picked up his shirt from a welter of clothes on a nightstand.

"You'll have to excuse me. Duty calls, and all that rot."

Quickly Holten dressed and left the room.

With the excitement of a schoolgirl, Rachel rolled over in bed and reached for a thick, leatherbound journal and a stub of yellow pencil. In a neat, precise script, she began to compose in the flamboyant style of the *Boston Herald*.

Upon arrival at Fort Rawlins, Dakota Territory, this reporter fell in with the brave and resourceful Chief Scout of the Twelfth Cavalry, Eli Holten. As a member in good standing of the "Cavalry Supporters' League," this reporter has been promised by that intrepid frontiersman to be taken to the very depths of the wilderness in search of bandits and savages. The next entry in this journal shall be from the field, with the fighting men of the valorous Twelfth . . .

Chapter 3

Not all of the Sioux ran wild across the high plains or hunted the forests and rivers of the woodlands. Some had accepted, with stoic resignation, the ways of the white farmers. They wore white man's clothing, their children attended schools run by whites, and they drew their regular allotments from the reservation agents. They had, to all outward appearances, become civilized. Their niggardly forty-acre farmsteads boasted small houses, usually constructed of lodge-pole pines and native mud, plus tidy barns and neat storage sheds. At one spot, near the fork of the Cheyenne and Belle Fourche Rivers, a little community had grown up. Near midnight, two days following the attack on Breakneck Gap, Freddy Mullins crouched beside his ground-reined horse and studied the Sioux Village as it lay basking in the light of a full moon.

"There it is, boys," he announced in a gruff whisper. "We hit this place first, then move on to the farms. Remember, Cap'n Weatherby wants us to bring in lots of young girls for the whorehouses."

"How young?" one hardbitten former foretopman inquired.

"If the sap runs outta the crack, she's old enough, I'd say," Mullins informed him. "Then we're gonna burn this heathen town to the ground."

"What if we get enough of these Injuns hot at us to start an uprising?" another dark face among the ten volunteers wanted to know.

"That's the Army's lookout, not ours. The main thing is to get the women an' liquor an' burn out the rest. Those redsticks oughta be snoozin' right good now, so let's get a move on."

Abandoning all caution, the eleven revenge hunters streaked down the shallow hillside toward the slumbering village. A few dogs yapped defensively and a man called out sleepily. Then the first shots slapped through oilcloth-covered windows and began to shatter dishware inside the nearer cabins.

Women shrieked and babies began to cry. Voices, shouting in Lakota, rose in confusion. A lantern went on in one building, only to be shot out by a charging hardcase. Two villagers, once warriors, now grown fat and slow on the white man's starchy food and an overabundance of liquor, stepped into the street and raised small-bore hunting rifles.

One died, screaming, with a pair of .44-40 slugs in his gut. The other, across the street, cleared a Breakneck Gap resident from the saddle with a sizzling round from a .32-20 Winchester. The half-naked Sioux dropped to one knee as a bullet burned a painful path across the top of his left shoulder. Quickly he raised the little weapon again and sighted on the man in the lead.

A slug cracked past Freddy Mullins' head. Reflexively, he bobbed to one side and sought the man who had fired on him. The shift in weight threw his striving mount off balance and it slewed around to the side, its chest crashing into the 4-by-4 upright of a porch roof.

The sunshade came down in a shower of shake shingles that knocked Freddy off his horse to roll painfully over the rough ground. By that time, the blazing guns of his companions had taken a frightful toll among the residents of the Sioux village.

Only three men, forted up behind a low stone wall, offered any resistance. Already some of the Breakneck Gap boys had begun to kick open doors and drag out screaming girls, ranging in age from eight to seventeen. Freddy came to his feet and looked around. Two men charged at the last defenders.

"Blast 'em!" Freddy called encouragement. "Get them red niggers!"

"They's pretty well protected," one gunslick protested.

"Well, shit, get around back of 'em," Freddy declared the obvious.

A moment later, Freddy saw movement as a brave exposed himself to get a clear shot. The Colt .45 in Freddy's right hand bucked and bellowed, and the slug sped to its destination. The Sioux gave a little grunt of pain and fell out of sight. Shots erupted from behind the wall.

"We got 'em! We got 'em all!" a triumphant voice yelled.

"Good. Now let's round up these females and get the hell outta here. Jory, Clem, you boys start settin' fire to these buildings."

"Mother, there's someone out there," eight-year-old Jason White Bear insisted, his eyes wide with excitement.

"It's only your imagination," his mother, *Susweca*, responded in Lakota. "Ever since your father left two days ago for the agent's office, you've seen bears and wolves and white pony-soldiers behind every tree."

"No. *Hecitu yelo*. There *is* someone out by the barn. White men."

Dragonfly stooped to comfort her son when the oil-cloth covering in the single window ripped open to a blast from a shotgun. A flaming torch followed. Jason White Bear screamed and ran for the small rabbit bow he had hanging beside the hearth. He had made only three steps when the door flew open and a big, burly white man with a scraggly beard stood on the threshold.

Casually Freddy Mullins eared back the hammer of his Colt and squeezed off a round. The bullet entered under Jason's left shoulderblade and burst outward from his chest in a shower of blood, bone chips and lung tissue. *Susweca* attacked the intruder with a large butcher knife.

A hot line seared across Freddy's neck and shoulder, and he spun to smash the smoking barrel of his revolver into the side of the Indian woman's head. Her eyes rolled up, and she slumped onto a buffalo robe that lay before the fireplace.

"Hell," Freddy called out to the others. "There ain't no younguns in here. Just one woman and a boy brat."

"What 're we gonna do, then?" Clem demanded in a whiny voice.

"Cut their throats and set this place on fire," Freddy answered.

Nate Applegate couldn't understand why it was they had to keep their hands off these Injun gals. What the hell was so special about takin' 'em back to Breakneck Gap without samplin' the wares? They *was* Injun gals, weren't they? Probably been fuckin' since they was old

30

enough to toddle away from their mammy's cradle boards. Leastwise that was what ever'body said about 'em.

Screw you like a mink. There was this one, in particular. Nice fat tits, all solid and pointy, good body under that thin dress. She must be all of sixteen. Plenty ripe and ready, to Nate's way of seein' things.

Nate reached down and rubbed at the swelling in the crotch of his trousers. 'T'weren't fair, leavin' him to watch all these pretty teases while the other boys hit a new Injun place they came across. What did Freddy expect him to be? Certain sure he had no monk's blood in him. He knew he had to ease the pressure somehow.

The buttons of his fly parted and his swollen, reddened penis swung into view. Most of the Sioux girls turned away, some shrunk back from his nearness. Not the perky one he'd been eyein', though, Nate noticed with rising ardor. She looked at his rod just bold as brass, while he stroked it. Bet she'd love to get a little of that. He rose up on his knees and waggled his turgid member close by her face.

"You like that, honey-chile?"

Smiling, she leaned forward and opened wide her small mouth. A flash of white, even teeth showed a moment before she took the tip of Nate's pulsing cock inside.

"Oh-boy-oh!" Nice exclaimed aloud. "I got me one o' them turkey gobblers. Well, you can take all of my turkey neck, sweetie pie."

That's when the Sioux girl bit him.

Nate screamed in horrified agony while she crunched down with all her might. The muscles of her jaws bulged under the bronze skin, and she exerted greater effort.

31

She had her determination rewarded when she felt her upper and lower teeth grind together.

Nate's blood spurted in her face as she spat out the quivering, severed glans and jumped back from the man before her. Nate howled in numbed terror, his mind teetering on the edge of insanity as he gazed in stunned disbelief at his maimed organ. Pain quickly made it go slack, though that did not lessen the steady carmine flow. Even as he watched the vicious young Indian begin to free the bonds of the others, he swayed from side to side, and his vision fuzzed over. Dizziness replaced the shock that had paralyzed him and he reeled about, still on his knees. Fighting encroaching darkness, Nate blinked his eyes.

Somehow, seemingly by magic, when Nate opened his eyes again, all of the Sioux girls had disappeared. Dimly Nate heard hoofbeats and angry shouts. Then screams and the sounds of struggling, as the boys from Breakneck Gap rounded up the fugitive captives.

The noise blended with the roaring inside his ears and became the last thing Nate Applegate heard on this earth.

"Jesus Christ!" Clem exclaimed when he discovered Nate's corpse, lying in a pool of blood.

"Bit the head clean off his pecker," Jory declared in an awed tone.

"Musta been this one with the bloody face," Freddy told the others.

"We oughta string her up!" Clem suggested hotly.

"Naw. Not her," Freddy refused. "One with that kind of spirit should make a mighty good saddle for a long day's ride. We'll take her back and let ol' 'Long Tom' Decker have a go at her. He'll break her to harness in no time."

Ben Nolte puckered his lips and gave a low whistle. "Who'd ever believe eleven inches of swingin' meat? 'Long Tom' sure deserves his name."

"He's calmed down more 'an one spitfire the Cap'n's brought in to Breakneck," Freddy allowed. "We'd best bury Nate an' head on. There's more places to hit."

"Sit down, Eli," General Frank Corrington told the scout when he entered the squadron commander's office.

Eli noted that the decanter of brandy had already been put out and the humidor of cigars on the general's desk stood invitingly open. Yep. This had to be another ball-breaker of an assignment.

"I summoned you here from more, ah, pleasant endeavors to offer you an extremely important assignment."

"Go on, Frank. I'm all ears."

Corrington raised a hand in mild protest. "No call for sarcasm, Eli. Things have been rather peaceful lately, haven't they?"

"We just passin' the time of day?"

"Hurrmph. I only sought to make an observation. Let me get right to the point. Intelligence sources have developed information regarding a hidden community right in the middle of the Black Hills. A couple of my informants allege that it is a town run by and for criminals. It is located in a ridge-locked valley that, legend has it, was formed by a meteor. There's only one narrow, twisting trail in or out." The general paused a moment to let this information sink in. He stroked long, spatulate fingers over his gracefully curved walrus mus-

33

tache and licked full, sensual lips. His light blue eyes flicked to the sideboard where the brandy waited.

"Worse, it seems that this place, Breakneck Gap, is located on the exact spot that has been chosen by the Sioux for this year's Sun Dance."

"Shit!" Eli exploded.

"Precisely. Perhaps you will join me in a small glass of brandy?"

"I think I'm gonna need the whole bottle before I hear the rest of this."

General Corrington gave the scout a wintry smile. "During the past year some time, since the last pow-wow, the town simply sprung up. The honor of selecting a site for the ritual went to the Sans Arc sub-group for this year. Kicking Elk, the over-all war leader of the Sans Arc, had a vision. The word has already gone out to all the Sioux. Before another two weeks, they will be packed up, lodges, dogs, kids, and all, and headed toward what they call the Valley-Where-the-Sky-Fell. Word has reached me that Kicking Elk has come back to scout out the location for the Sun Dance.

"When he finds out about Breakneck Gap, if he hasn't already, he will lead his people—and any other Sioux who will follow—in a crusade to drive every offending white man from anywhere within miles of the sacred Black Hills."

"He'll have plenty of help in that," Eli opined, considering the gloomy news the general had given him.

"Only too true. Particularly since I have another bit of news. Most disturbing at that. White men have been attacking peaceful Sioux, on and off the reservation. They kill the men and burn homes. They also abduct all of the women under the age of twenty or so. From what survivors have said, including two girls who escaped from their captors, this is being done by the same motley ne'er-do-wells and border ruffians who inhabit Breakneck Gap."

"If that's the case, it could bring on a general uprising of all the Sioux," Eli remarked, agitated.

Corrington nodded. He reached out and poured more brandy for them both. "I'm putting two companies of the Twelfth in the field. I want you to scout for them. Their mission is to make their way to Breakneck Gap, free of any Sioux women held captive there, and any other hostages, then clean out that rat's nest of thieves and killers. It is to be accomplished as swiftly as possible, before Kicking Elk starts a general slaughter that would wipe out every white person in the Territory and a few neighboring states."

Eli Holten half rose. "I can be ready to leave within an hour."

"I thought you would see it my way, Eli," General Corrington returned. "I've taken the liberty of notifying Captain Pierce and his subordinates. The column will be outfitted and mounted within an hour and a half. And . . . good luck, Eli."

Five excited men jumped up and down and slapped each other on the back. Gleeful voices shouted back and forth as one man cavorted with a gold pan over his head. Their presence in this portion of the Sioux treaty lands of the Black Hills was strictly illegal. That made no difference to them.

"It's the mother lode!" one prospector howled in delight.

"By dang, we've struck it rich!" another bellowed.

35

"I'm gonna make me a shithouse of solid gold bricks!" a third declared.

Gold, a rich, tempting strike that took away all their cares.

They didn't worry, but the fifteen braves with Stone Heart growled with discontent as they watched the cavorting white men below them. From the brow of a small ridge, the Sans Arc warriors observed and muttered angrily among themselves.

"We will kill them all," Stone Heart told his followers. "Take their scalps to Kicking Elk."

A moment later, they attacked. The prospectors shouted and ran for their weapons. One, drawing his revolver from its soft leather holster, stood in midstream and fired his cylinder dry at the charging Sioux while his comrades stumbled onto the bank and sought protection, hands grasping rifles in panicked haste.

Blood flew from the rear guard's back. Three arrows plunked into his chest with meaty smacks, the tips shoving out the heavy leather of his vest. He staggered and fell. The corpse, half submerged, floated undisturbed downstream. Angry yells came from his companions, who opened fire on the attacking braves.

Another of the angered and worried miners fired both barrels of a shotgun at point blank range into a plunging, rearing horse. The wounded animal reared and pitched over backward, pinning the helpless rider beneath its weight, crushing bone and flesh.

Suddenly a warbling cry came from above.

At once the warriors broke off their attack and rode beyond the far bank of the stream. A minute later, Kicking Elk and several of his followers rode into sight. He closed the distance to his trusted lieutenant and greeted him warmly.

"It is good to run the seekers of yellow metal from our sacred hills. But now is not the time to start a general killing of whites. We must wait for a while. In a dream I saw the pony-soldiers fighting their own kind. We should let those at the fort lodges of the soldiers know what is going on. Tell them of the shiny gun that shoots far off and the men who have dishonored the treaty and our land."

"Why is this, brother?"

"It is as I saw it, Stone Heart. Take that one over there, the white who bleeds from his arm. Give him his horse. Also give him a message. If the whites do not get the bad men out of the Valley-Where-the-Sky-Fell, the Dakota will kill every white we can find."

Stone Heart attempted to explain about the Whitworth Rifles and the men violating the treaty in the small valley. His command of English went little beyond ordering coffee, sugar, whiskey and ammunition. Confused and weakened by blood loss, the surviving miner couldn't be considered in a receptive mood. What he did understand, he didn't retain for long. All he knew was that for some damnfool reason, this high muckety-muck Injun would give him his life back if he rode like hell to the cavalry.

That was inducement enough.

Chapter 4

Capt. Anthony Pierce, commanding officer of B Company of the Twelfth Cavalry, and First Lieutenant Edward Holland, CO of Company D, stood conferring with the regimental commander, Colonel Dobbs, and General Corrington. Drawn up on foot, in four ranks each, the two companies of troops waited restlessly on the parade ground, hands to the headstalls of their matched bays. Eli Holten led his Morgan stallion over to a tie-rail near the officers and joined their conversation.

"Good you're here, Eli," the general greeted.

"Ready any time," the scout handed back.

"This outlaw town is supposed to be right in the dead center of the Black Hills," the general went on. "How do you propose to approach it?"

"I think we should skirt the Badlands to the north, come in on the road to Deadwood," Eli suggested. "Then cut southwest through the hills until we come on the valley. I've heard of it, but never seen the place. Next to the caves to the south, this is the most sacred part of the *hesapa* to the Sioux and Cheyenne. Having white men build any sort of town there could put us up to our elbows in shit."

"If you've never been there, scout, how can you lead our troops to this place?" Lieutenant Holland inquired in a haughty, somewhat condescending voice.

Edward Holland, scion of a wealthy Eastern family, considered most men beneath him. He had wealth, position and, unfortunately to his way of seeing things, a tradition of service to the country that went back generations. Save but for that, he would be enjoying a sail off Martha's Vineyard right now, or assuming a place of importance on the board of any one of a dozen companies owned by his father and uncles. Newly promoted, he had been transferred to the frontier despite vociferous protests by his influential male parent and himself. Washington was the place for him. He had no intention of disrupting his carefully planned future with a Sioux arrow.

Despite the pressures brought to bear, the pundits of the War Department and the Army of the West prevailed. Lieutenant Edward Holland went first to Jefferson Barracks, Missouri, and then by way of sidewheeler steam packet to Dakota Territory. His resentment of this, to him, cavalier treatment spilled over into his attitude toward his brother officers, his subordinate noncoms, troopers, and all civilians.

Eli Holten's eyes narrowed at the slighting remark. "That's an interesting question from someone who can't find his butt with a bullfiddle once he's out of sight of the fort."

Holland bristled immediately. "If you were any sort of gentleman, I would challenge you for that remark, scout."

General Corrington loudly cleared his throat. "Let me remind you, Lieutenant, that as Chief Scout, Mr.

Holten holds a rank equivalent to major. In future, I would suggest you use the proper term of address to him — which is, in case you have forgotten, *sir.*"

"Yes, sir," Holland returned as he stiffened to the position of attention. "My apologies, Mr. Holten, *sir.*"

"In the field, call me Eli," the scout said offhandedly. "I haven't been 'sir-ed' a dozen times in my life. And then by far better men than yourself, Lieutenant."

A frosty silence held a moment. Colonel Dobbs verbally stepped into the breach. "See to your troops, gentlemen. Mr. Holten, a word with you, please?"

As the young officers turned to confer with their troop sergeants, Colonel Dobbs walked aside with Eli Holten. "Lieutenant Holland doesn't belong here. We all know that. He resents this assignment, whether rightly or wrongly, I don't know. If that sounds contradictory, it isn't meant to.

"On the one hand, as a soldier, he must do his duty. That means taking his assignments as they are handed out and making the most he can of them. On the other hand, he is so obviously a misfit on the frontier. It is my hope that this tour of duty will make a fine officer of him. Whether or not it does, we still have to live with him, at least until he is transferred somewhere else. Try to get along. I recommended to the general that his troop be included in this foray. It might give him a better sense of perspective."

"I appreciate that, Colonel. Green officers are a burden at best. One with a chip on his shoulder can be the start of a tragedy. What I'm saying is that I don't like to have to watch my back in hostile country."

"You can count on Captain Pierce. He's steady. He knows Indians and he can deal tactfully or ruthlessly with the sort of frontier scum you're likely to encounter in this unauthorized town. Rely on him."

"I will, sir. Now, we had better get on the way."

"Quite so. Good luck, Mr. Holten."

A brief, amused smile flickered at the corners of Eli's mouth. "That's what General Corrington said. This task must be a bitch to higher command."

Eli turned to go. A bull-like roar from the porch in front of the sutler's store halted him in midstride.

"There's that sumbitch now!"

A giant of a man, dressed in grease-stained buckskins, knee-high moccasins and a large, floppy, once-gray felt hat, swayed drunkenly on the edge of the plank-floored porch. Beady, close-set eyes showed red-rimmed and watery. One hand clutched the wooden haft of a large Russel Green River knife thrust into a wide leather belt that bound his huge expanse of belly. The other unsteadily brandished a cocked, fully-loaded Prescott .44 Army revolver.

"I come to get you, Holten, you bastard!" the intoxicated behemoth bellowed.

Memory stirred vaguely for Eli Holten. A face, younger though similar to the one before him, came into shape. Then a name. Brockman . . . Clell Brockman.

Some two years earlier, Eli Holten had been scouting for a small punitive expedition against a dozen hothead braves who had jumped the Pine Ridge reservation. He had come upon a large, prosperous-looking soddy while it was in the process of being robbed. The owner sprawled in the yard in a pool of blood. His wife lay on the bed, amid the disarray of her dress and petticoats, fighting valiantly to prevent the painful indignity of rape.

Three young toughs, the oldest not more than nineteen, ranged about her, trousers open, swollen organs exposed and ready. As the woman screamed for mercy, Holten had taken a hand.

"Hold it, you three," the scout commanded, Remington ready in his fist.

The trio of would-be badmen had not exercised good sense.

Resenting the sudden interference, they had attempted to remove its cause.

Eli shot one of them through the shoulder. He would later keep a date with the hangman for his deeds, the scout recalled. The other two proved less easy to subdue.

The oldest whirled with a snarl, hand clawing for his six-gun. Eli shot him twice, the bullets forming a perfect figure eight two inches above and to the right of his navel. Hot lead destroyed his liver and one kidney, and the amateur hardcase turned into a corpse before he hit the floor.

That left the remaining youthful bandit. Pale-skinned and scarred with pimples, he decided to eliminate the woman first, since she represented the only witness outside of this interfering stranger. He counted on his partners to exterminate the latter threat. He learned the error of his ways and his plans when a sizzling .44 slug smashed through his temple and jellied his brain.

His eyes bulged, and one popped free of its socket to dangle on his cheek, held by the severely strained optic nerve. Clell Brockman had been his name, the scout learned later. Seventeen years old and one of a brood of eleven boys in the Brockman family. Right at that moment, though, he was only another piece of dead meat. Over the eventful months since, the scout had forgotten the incident. At least until this much larger edition of the Brockman clan appeared so menacingly on the sutler's porch.

"Y'don't know me, Holten," the threatening man slurred. "But I know you. You did in my baby brother, Clell Brockman. 'Member the name? Now you're gonna get yours."

"You're drunk, Brockman," Holten said levelly. "Put away the weapons before the Provost Marshal has you hauled to the stockade."

"We Brockmans take care of our own," the inebriated man persisted as though he had not heard the remark. "We figger to hang you, you rotten bastard."

"Corporal of the guard, Post Number One!" the sentry outside the headquarters building sang out. "Armed aggressor at the sutler's store."

"Shut up, sonny, or you'll catch the first bullet," Brockman snarled.

Swiftly Eli evaluated the situation, gauged the distance and reliability of his ammunition, the time he had to draw. As Brockman turned his attention to the young private on guard duty, the scout's Remington cleared leather.

Holten's first bullet caught Brockman in the right shoulder. He howled more in rage than pain, and his ancient, well-worn revolver thudded on the plank flooring. Immediately he drew his knife left-handed and leaped down onto the parade ground.

A second round belched from the Remington held steadily in Holten's right hand. The slug smashed off the zyphoid process from the tip of Brockman's sternum.

43

Bone chips sprayed his lungs, yet the monster kept coming. Crimson froth flecked his lips as he staggered toward Eli Holten. Lifting the revolver in both hands to eye level, the scout cocked it again and fired a third shot.

Hot lead drilled a neat round hole in the center of Brockman's massive forehead. His head snapped backward, and he came to a sudden halt. Slowly he began to wilt.

"Yu-you . . . done . . . kilt . . . me . . ." he gasped out a moment before he crumpled to the ground. His knife lay only two feet from Holten's tense, straining body.

"Christ!" Lieutenant Holland gushed in an awed whisper to his troop sergeant. "I'd never want Holten mad at me."

"Sure an' yer learning the ropes right well, Lieutenant," Sergeant Mallory replied through a grin.

Still tingling and burning inside from the marvelous lovemaking of Eli Holten, Rachel Johnson urged her gentle mount forward, reins in her left hand, as she rode sidesaddle onto the parade ground. Although her journal rested secure in a pocket of her voluminous riding skirt, Rachel busily composed lines in her mind as she took in the activity attendant to the expedition's departure.

Amidst the controlled bustle of activity the gallant men in blue make ready to sally out against the enemy. This time their destination is an infamous outlaw stronghold known as Breakneck Gap. Horses are saddled, weapons checked a final time, and the waggoners inspect their precious cargoes of grain for the horses, food and ammunition for the men. While this occurs, the dashingly handsome Colonel addresses his junior officers, with the assistance of the intrepid scout, Eli Holten. When all is in readiness, the command to mount is given and eighty-six . . . no, ninety-three men swing into the saddle.

The sudden disturbance at the sutler's caught her unprepared. She reined in sharply and watched in startled absorption as the drunken Brockman challenged Holten. He looked so formidable standing on the porch, weapons at the ready. Her heart thudded with anxiety for Eli.

Then Eli shot Brockman in the shoulder.

For a moment, Rachel thought she would faint. She had never seen a man struck by a bullet before. The second wound Brockman received from the scout nearly finished her. She swayed in the saddle and rapidly blinked her eyes in an attempt to preserve her swimming vision. When Eli's third round dropped the pugnacious fellow, she nearly lost her breakfast. Then her reporter's instincts took control. She edged her horse closer to where several men gathered around Holten.

"Drag that body out of here," Holten told the corporal of the guard, who had arrived with three men as unneeded reinforcements.

"You'll be required to make the identification and file a report, Mister Holten," the NCO told him.

"After we get back. He won't keep, but that will. I'd recommend he be buried deep, in an unmarked grave. There's nine more Brockman boys, and every one of them with a criminal record."

"No loss," Captain Pierce remarked as he looked down at the corpse. "Fortunate for you, Eli, that this will have cooled off by the time we get back."

"Will it, Tony?"

"Was it entirely necessary to resort to killing that

45

man?" Rachel inquired when she could get Holten's attention. "Surely you could have reasoned with him?"

Eli looked up and saw her for the first time. "I did reason with him, Miss Johnson. Only *he* lost the debate. Now, could you tell me what it is you're up to this morning?"

Aghast at his rude directness, Rachel gasped. "Why, I'm coming along, of course."

"No, you're not."

"I certainly am," Rachel responded, aggressively thrusting her chin into the air. "What was our, ah, interview all about last night if not this?"

"It surely wasn't about a young woman going along on a mission as touchy as this."

Rachel's temper flared. "Now you see here, Mr. Eli Holten. I came out here to do a story. I can't do that from inside the walls of Fort Rawlins. This expedition of yours is an ideal means for me to get what I want."

"You're not going! It's much too dangerous."

"I'll be the judge of that."

"You won't have the opportunity."

"You can't interfere with the freedom of the press," Rachel challenged. "Our readers have a right to know what the Army is doing out here."

"Take it up with General Corrington," Eli snapped. He suddenly realized that the gathered officers and noncoms were immensely enjoying this heated conversation.

"I thought we had a mission to undertake," he growled in the direction of Captain Pierce.

"So we do," came the officer's amused reply. "Sergeant, mount the troops."

"Yes, sir. Bee Company . . . pre-pare to mount."

"Dee Company . . . pre-pare to mount" echoed the troop sergeant of Lieutenant Holland's command.

"Mount!"

"We're leaving now," Eli told a spluttering Rachel. "I'd suggest you make yourself comfortable until we return. I promise to tell you all about it."

"You men — you — you make me furious."

"But you're not going along."

"Try and stop me."

"Soldier," Eli cracked at the sentry outside headquarters. "There's an unauthorized person on your post. I suggest you inform the corporal of the guard and have her removed to the provost's office until this column is well out of sight of the fort."

"Yes, sir. As you say, sir." He came forward and firmly grasped the headstall of Rachel's horse.

"Beast!" Rachel wailed as the scout took his place beside Captain Pierce.

"Column of twos to the left . . . ho!" Sergeant McNiel commanded.

"Look who's here!" Sylvia Vickers cried excitedly as an attractive young woman walked through the batwing doors of the Thunder Saloon in Eagle Pass.

"Hello, girls," Mrs. Amy Smith called pleasantly as she strode further into the big room of the main bar. "I had to come in for some yardgoods I ordered, so I thought I'd drop by for a little chat."

Like a covey of hungry quail, Amy's former co-workers swarmed around her, with hugs and pecks on the cheek. Amy returned their embraces delightedly. The questions flowed like the peeps of hungry chicks.

"How's the farm?"

"How's the new church coming?"

"Are you in a family way yet?"

"Do you miss us?"

"Have you seen that divine Eli Holten?"

"Is your husband with you?"

"Wait. Wait, girls. I can only answer one at a time," Amy laughingly protested. "First off, the farm is wonderful. We have new piglets, two hens are brooding, and there's one hatch of chicks already. Ezekiel is painting the barn. And as for the church, one of the things I came to tell you is that there will be a bellraising this next Sunday. Basket supper to follow. The new pews will be here within two weeks from Kansas City."

A chorus of excited chatter and speculation drowned her out for a while. Amy took the opportunity to remove her bonnet and reveal her luxurious blonde hair. It fell in thick tresses from her well-formed head and made shining waves as it spilled over her shoulders. Sparkling blue eyes twinkled with merriment. She looked beyond her friends and saw over the batwings a young face that could have been pretty, if not so distorted by hatred. Whatever could such an attractive child be so disdainful of, Amy wondered.

Elizabeth Brewster had been arrested in her progress along the plankwalk by the talk of church emanating from inside the Thunder Saloon. Astonished at this incongruity, she had remained to listen further. She knew the Reverend Ezekiel Smith, of course. Everyone in Eagle Pass did. She also knew, and heartily disapproved, of his wife's former occupation. What a horrid, sinful town Eagle Pass had turned out to be.

At the ripe age of fifteen, quite prim and proper, her maidenhead still intact and waiting for Mr. Appropriate, Elizabeth Brewster could afford the luxury of over-weening self-righteousness. How could any man of the cloth marry a—a *tainted woman*? She had asked herself that question often during the month her family had stayed in Eagle Pass awaiting the soon-to-be discharge of her elder brother from the cavalry, so they could go on to civilized living in San Francisco.

How glad she would be when she at last departed this hotbed of sin for the glamor of California. At least she knew better than these soiled drabs who seemed to surround her in Eagle Pass. Virtue was its own reward. Wouldn't it be nice if something *dreadful* happened to them all? Sort of God's punishment for their flagrant breaking of His commandments.

Chapter 5

Freddy Mullins squatted on the dry, hard earth of the hillside to the west of the small community. He had been the one to suggest to Captain Weatherby that a bit of variety was needed among the painted ladies who occupied the three bordellos in Breakneck Gap. Naturally the Captain had put him in charge of providing the new blood, so to speak.

"White women?" the former Royal Navy officer had remarked. "What a bloody novelty that would be. See to it, Mr. Mullins, will you? Bring us these girls you know of."

"Aye-aye, sir. It will certainly be appreciated by us who live here all the time. Injun women are all right for the fellers passing through, but we could use the change."

"Capital. Arrange it for the last part of your sweep through the 'civilized' Sioux."

And so he was here. From this distance, Eagle Pass didn't look like much. Having been there, he knew it wasn't. But it did have a supply of young and tasty females. They could take their pick. The last time Freddy had been in Eagle Pass, the town marshal had just been gunned down by a young holdup artist. Without law, or at least with only some badge-packer chosen from the other residents of the town, they should have an easy time. When the rest of his men arrived with their Indian captives, he would set up a means of gathering all the tender rosebuds they could manage.

Rachel Johnson took iron control of her racing emotions. She looked speculatively at the pink-cheeked recruit who had been detailed to contain her. This, she thought, would be like taking candy from a trusting child.

"Soldier," she cooed, "I gather that you are rather new in the Army."

"Yes, ma'am. I came out here only a month ago from Jefferson Barracks."

"I'm sure the readers of my newspaper, the *Boston Herald*, would be delighted to hear your impressions of frontier service. You've heard of our paper, haven't you?"

"Oh, no, ma'am. I'm from Waycross, Georgia, myself. We don't see many dam . . . uh, Yankee newspapers in those parts." His guileless gray eyes shone with innocence under a mop of flaxen hair and matching brows.

"Well then, this will be quite an experience for you. If I'm going to interview you, I'm sure we would be more comfortable in the quarters assigned to me."

"I ain't sure Sergeant Kaufmann would approve of that, ma'am."

"So long as you fulfill your assignment of keeping me on the post, what possible objection can there be? Come on. What is your name, by the way?"

"Andrews, ma'am. Pa — Patrick. Only my friends call me, ah, Andy."

Once inside her small cabin, Rachel unfastened the top two buttons of her riding habit. "This costume is so uncomfortable in a confined space." Swiftly she undid the remaining ones and peeled out of her clothes. "Let me slip into something more comfortable."

Conversation inside the Thunder Saloon turned to womanly interests in fashion and new styles. As Sylvia and the other soiled doves extolled the virtues of the currently popular Eastern designers, three men ambled into the establishment and took places along the bar. They ordered drinks and silently went about a careful examination of the interior. Fascinated that these wretched examples of degraded womanhood could take interest in such subjects, Elizabeth Brewster lingered near the swinging doors to take in more of what was said.

While the chatter continued about hats and dresses, a light wagon, its size exaggerated by iron bow hoops and a canvas cover, rolled into the alley and stopped outside the rear entrance to the Thunder Saloon. Two men stepped down from the high seat. Without hesitation, they walked to the closed portal. One produced a short, curved steel bar. With it he forced the flimsy lock, and they hurried inside.

"Now, as to the church," Amy informed her onetime sisters in sin. "Ezekiel plans to build a school next. It will be on ground he owns beside the church. Before long, Eagle Pass will be a right proper town."

Two men rushed into the large room from the rear, knives glinting wickedly in their hands. Immediately, the trio at the bar drew their weapons and advanced on the two customers, the bartender and a gray-bearded swamper who was industriously polishing spittoons.

"You ladies stay where you are," a tall, lean man wearing a fur cap directed them.

Swiftly the male occupants of the Thunder Saloon died from expertly placed knife strokes. Two of the soiled doves squealed in horror and another turned away to retch. Amy Smith rose in anger, her fists clenched.

"Stop it, honey. You've got to be the prettiest one here. No call to spoil all that tasty stuff, is there?" one ugly bandit sneered.

"Hey, Freddy," a sixth hardcase called from the front entrance. "Lookie what I found. Another sweet li'l dove for our nest."

"Let me go! Take your filthy hands off of me," Elizabeth Brewster shouted as the tough lifted her off her feet and hustled her inside. "I — I'm not one — one of *them*!"

"Well, sister, you sure as hell are gonna be," Freddy Mullins laughingly told her as he reached out and tweaked one small, firm breast.

Elizabeth writhed away from him, her face black with loathing, though a white ring around her mouth betrayed her fear.

Swiftly the soiled doves of the Thunder Saloon had their hands bound and mouths covered by strips of cloth that effectively gagged them. The motley crew hustled them out the back way and into the wagon. Among them went Amy Smith, wife of the Reverend Ezekiel Smith and friend of Eli Holten.

In the narrow, down-comforter-covered bed, Rachel Johnson squealed with delight at the rough, inexperienced thrusting as young Trooper Andrews drove his rigid phallus deeply into her sodden nest. She hooked her legs over his narrow waist and drove her heels into his buttocks. It increased by at least two inches the piercing of his driving shaft.

"That's it. Oooh, yes-yes-yes! Deeper! Harder! Faster!" she cried out.

Rachel ruffled his shock of tow-hair with one hand while she used the other to cup his large, hairy scrotum. She could feel his heart thudding in his bare chest, and it increased the speed of her own. Amazed to discover that he was a virgin, she had first knelt before his naked form and flicked out her tongue to savor the sweetness of his untried manhood.

Andy had shivered with delight at this contact and eagerly awaited more as she moved closer and let her silken lips caress the sensitive flesh of his hot, raging staff. Anxious to please and be pleased, Rachel gave it her all. Before he could explode, though, she had hurried him into bed.

Now Andy groaned with unfathomable delight as his moment arrived and he catapulted over the edge into sensual oblivion. His jerks and shudders only aroused his partner the more.

"Oh, Andy, Andy. This has been some interview," Rachel panted as they wound down from their mutual fulfillment. "I just know the readers will be assured by my account of the strength and endurance of our soldier boys on the frontier. Even though they may lack a little, uh, something in experience. Now, as to my staying in this dull old place, instead of going out where the action is . . . ?"

"G-g-go on. I couldn't stop you if I wanted to. I'm so weak I can't stand."

Rachel bent down and kissed the reddened weapon with which Andy had fought such a valiant battle. "You're a dear, dear boy, Andy. I knew you'd give me what I needed." *In more ways than one*, she thought with dreamy satisfaction.

Only a few brief moments went by before the crime in the Thunder Saloon became known to all of Eagle Pass. A young lad was sent to inform the Reverend Smith, who appeared in his clerical garb, a brown leather cartridge belt around his waist, from which was holstered an oiled and well-used .45 Colt.

"The Lord commands us to defend our homes and families. Come, brothers, let us go get what is ours." Heavenly wrath blazed in his dark eyes, and his bushy brows waggled as he spoke. His wide shoulders and the long, muscular arms which bulged in the black parson's coat seemed incongruous on a clerical man, as did the hard, square jaw and the firm set of this thin lips.

Led by the fiery man of God, the menfolk of Eagle Pass stormed after the fleeing miscreants. They rode for an hour before spotting a column of dust on the horizon.

"There they are!" Ezekiel declared. "We'll be on them within an hour. Free our women, but take no prisoners. The Lord can sort out the ones worthy of salvation from the rest."

Freddy Mullins had wisely appointed one man as rear guard. He spotted the approach of the angry posse from Eagle Gap in time to warn the slowmoving wagons and the men who guarded them. As the avengers thundered down, Winchesters and Colts blazing, the outlaw band returned a withering fire.

Few bullets from either side struck home. One Eagle

Pass merchant received a flesh wound in his left arm, and a horse got shot from under Eb Tyson. In the midst of the foray, a voice called out from among the bandits.

"Hold yer fire, dang it. If you men don't back off, we'll butcher these women like hogs in a slaughterhouse."

"Stop shooting, men," Ezekiel commanded, his mind on his lovely wife. "I have a feeling he means what he says. Who are you?"

"None of your nevermind. We got the women. They don't mean anything to us. You all pull back an' let us go, or they die. One . . . by . . . one."

"All right. We agree," the Reverend Smith acknowledged. To the others, he quietly added, "We'll leave a few back on the trail a ways. Let them dog this bunch to wherever it goes. In the meanwhile, I'm going after Eli Holten."

Afternoon had worn down its edge when Eli Holten returned to the column from a long scout ahead. His features remained impassive, though a grim light glowed in his eyes.

"Captain, I need a bit of assistance up ahead. There's a problem with the terrain."

"That's easy to take care of. Sergeant—"

"It would help if you came yourself, Captain," Eli interrupted.

Pierce took the hint and nodded. "Sergeant McNiel, you'll accompany the scout and myself. Lieutenant Holland, you are in charge. Give the men ten minutes to cool out their horses. And smoke, if they've got the makings."

"Yes, sir."

Over a distant swale, where the prairie surrendered

to the Black Hills, Eli led Captain Pierce and his sergeant to the grisly scene. Bloody and begrimed, a raggedly dressed prospector lay panting feebly on the ground. Eli nodded to the man as they dismounted.

"Says he has a message for the Army. A message from Kicking Elk. Thought you'd want to hear it privately first."

"Thank you, Eli." Pierce knelt beside the weakened miner and gently lifted his battered head. "What is it, man? What is your message?"

"Y-you the Army?"

"Yes. Tell me."

"We got jumped. Bunch of Sioux. Thought we was all goners, until this big chief rides up and stops the shootin'. Said his name was Kicking Elk. Wan-wanted me to take a message to Fort Rawlins."

"What is it Kicking Elk told you?" Pierce said earnestly.

"Said to let you know some white men had moved onto sacred ground of the Sioux. That if the Army didn't run them out, like the treaty said, then all whites around the Black Hills would die."

"Go on. Anything else?"

"N-no. Said a—a lot o' crazy things. About the Great Spirit an' a dream of his an then he—he started ravin' all wildlike. Didn't make no sense at all. Only—only that the Army had better chase the white-eyes out of some valley called Where-the-Sky-Fell."

Blood bubbled up in the miner's mouth. Internal injuries he had suffered before Kicking Elk arrived in the small mining camp had opened seeping wounds. A hollow rattle in his throat told Eli that the man had little time to live. The Sioux had not bothered to bandage his wounded arm.

"There has to be more to it than that. Why else would Kicking Elk bother to spare this one to send his message?" Captain Pierce speculated aloud.

"I don't know, Captain," Holten replied. "I suppose we'll find out when we catch up to Kicking Elk."

"First we have to deal with the whites in this Breakneck Gap place. If we run them out, Kicking Elk will be pacified."

"For the time being. The Sans Arc aren't reservation Indians. Anything might set them off between now and the end of the Sun Dance."

"I know that," Pierce snapped irritably. "Sorry, Eli. What about this one?"

"He's going to die." The scout looked down at the prospector. "It's not the Sioux who killed you. It's your own greed. These hills are supposed to be closed to prospecting and settlement. Deadwood got big too fast for the Army to do anything. But men like you—"

"I—I ain't gonna go alone. I spanged a couple of them damned redsticks."

"For which, if you weren't going to leak to death first, we could hang you. This is Indian land. Leave it the hell alone."

"Calm down, Eli. He ain't gonna bother anyone again," Captain Pierce advised, one hand resting on the scout's shoulder.

He knew of the years the scout had spent as a youth among the Oglala. To that very day, Holten remained known to the Sioux as Tall Bear. He had ridden with their warparties and hunted buffalo, elk, and bear beside them. His sympathies, at best, could be described as divided. After years of fruitless service on the frontier, the Captain wasn't all too sure he himself couldn't be considered the same way.

"Fuckin' . . . Injun . . . lover . . . ." the prospector choked out in red-frothed spurts. He shuddered violently, heels kicking the dirt, and died.

"We'll bury him ourselves and move on. No need for the troops to see this," Eli suggested. "They'd only want what he wanted."

"I know. Sometimes I wonder if we're on the right side out here, myself," Captain Pierce agreed.

Twenty minutes later, the shallow grave had been filled in and covered with a cairn of stones. Eli Holten and the captain; along with Sergeant McNiel, returned to the column, and they continued on toward the valley where William Weatherby had built his city of sin.

Chapter 6

The intrepid troopers from Companies B and D of the Twelfth Cavalry, along with yours truly, who was accepted as a brother in arms by the brave fellows of the Frontier Army, boldly challenged the wilderness, seeking out the evil miscreants of the Dakota Territory at a place called Breakneck Gap . . .

Rachel Johnson continued to compose her masterful series on the prairie army in her head. She lay on her stomach in the tall buffalo grass as she watched the punitive expedition through a pair of field glasses. Just to gaze at so many brawny, resourceful men made her itch. Lord, what a difference from those soft, self-deprecating Eastern sissies who worked for her father.

Norbert Denton Johnson owned an extensive chain of textile mills in the small towns outside Boston. His home on Beacon Hill rated as one of the largest and most opulently appointed. As his daughter, Rachel had enjoyed a sheltered childhood, one filled with every luxury. Not that her father tolerated her being cosseted.

Far from it. Norbert Johnson had early shown Rachel what life for the common mill workers was like. In her childish innocence, she had felt sorry for them and vowed that when she grew up, she would make their situation better. But she had always had the itch and, at age thirteen, when she at last scratched it, her overpowering libido got in the way of much of her idealism. Often, when she was grunting and sweating with one of her school friends whom she had enticed into the haymow of the family stable, she would fantasize that she was a poor mill girl, being taken advantage of by the lustful foreman. Later, the image changed to that of the mill owner. But through all the pains of adolescence, she maintained a strong belief that women should have the same freedoms in the workforce as men, and damn well have equal pay.

Such opinions didn't make her popular, but it did give her a certain tenacity and strength of character that served well in the competitive world of journalism. Her father believed her to be a secretary for the *Boston Herald*, an acceptable position for a woman in business. He would simply die if he could see her now, belly down on a rocky ridgeline in the Dakota Territory, wearing a mannish riding habit and following along behind two companies of cavalry. A moment passed in silent reflection, and then Rachel stirred, rising to hurry to her horse.

The cavalry had started to mount up. Quickly she formed new word images in her mind.

With flankers far out on all sides, the column formed under the broiling sun. In the lead are Captain Pierce and the bold scout, Eli Holten. Stalwartly they head out at the command to move forward. This reporter was privileged to ride along side these two accomplished frontiersm —

Rachel's narrative broke off after she had tightened her cinch and turned partway to step into the stirrup. When she did, she came face to face with two utterly nasty-looking Sans Arc warriors, who had already begun to reach for her. Idly, as the savages took her captive, she wondered if her copy would require much rewrite.

Freddy Mullins picked a location to stop for the night. No sooner had the small column halted, than he picked out one of the lush lovelies from the Thunder Saloon. He gathered her close to him and began to tear at her clothes.

"C'mere, me lovely," he panted. "We're gonna have us some fun."

From experience, Freddy knew that the best success could be derived from utter dominance at the earliest moment. The surest means to achieve that, he believed, was to start raping and terrorizing the captive women as quickly as possible. As the young prostitute struggled in his hands, Freddy had time to give attention to a conversation close at hand.

"But, I tell you, I'm not one of *them*. I don't belong here. You will simply have to take me back. I'm no whore," Elizabeth insisted pedantically. "I'm unsoiled, untouched."

"Hey, boys," Clem called out. "We've got us a virgin here. What do ya say about that?"

"I don't believe it," a reply came from the cookfire. "Hell, we caught her on her way into a bawdyhouse, didn't we? Maybe she's one of those who miraculously regrows her maidenhood after each fuck."

Lecherous laughter rose from the hardened outlaws.

"We can always see," Clem suggested. "If she does, she can make a fortune in Breakneck Gap."

"I knew a gal like that," Wendell Owens said wistfully.

"She had hot pants from the time she was a little tyke. I poked her for the first time the year before we got out of grade school. Ever' time after that, she'd always say, 'Please, please. Be gentle. I'm a virgin.'"

More lusty guffaws filled the camp.

"Oooh! You men are absolutely horrible. Why, every girl wants to save herself for that Special Man in her life."

"Honey," Clem cooed as he plucked at the ribbons on Elizabeth's dress, "you don't have to save it up any longer. I'm gonna be that 'Special Man' you're talkin' about."

Elizabeth screamed and tried to fight off the aroused man. Drumming hoofbeats, rather than her efforts, prevented Clem from claiming his prize.

"What's your big hurry, Joe?" Freddy inquired as the outrider surged into camp in a welter of dust.

"There's a big column of cavalry about ten miles from here. They're headed right for Breakneck Gap."

A shocked silence held for a moment. Then Freddy Mullins burst into motion. "Leave the wagons behind. We gotta mount these females up on the spare horses and head for the valley. Captain Weatherby has got to know of this right away."

Capt. William Weatherby sat at the dining table in the suite occupied by himself and his daughter in the Gold Coast, the largest of the three bordellos in Breakneck Gap. The remains of a roasted joint of mutton lay cooling in the congealing grease and pan drippings on a silver platter before him. He had eaten well. As usual, the noonday meal was his largest. Marilee had worked as overseer to the cook, who had done a fine job with roast potatoes, turnip greens, fresh bread and the divine leg of mutton. Weatherby's tongue flicked out and snared a stray bit of mint jelly at the corner of his mouth. He sighed contentedly and sipped from a crystal goblet of claret.

"A marvelous meal, my dear," he told his daughter.

"Thank you, Daddy. I saw to it that Cook did his best. I even promised, ah, that he might receive a little something special for a good job," she added amusedly.

"Promise not what is not yours to give away," the captain intoned in mock piety.

"Yes. I know. All I have belongs to my Daddy. Where did you send Freddy and the men?"

"On raids against the Sioux and to pick up some white women for our bordellos from a place he knows of."

"Do you think that wise?"

"White whores are not the Army's concern."

"I didn't mean them. If the Sioux get too angry, they might join together and come here to wipe us out."

"Marilee, Marilee, don't worry yourself over something so unlikely as that. The 'civilized' Sioux envy their free brothers, and the wild hostiles have nothing but contempt for the reservation creatures. They could never, ah, 'get together,' as you put it."

"What is it that we're building here, Father?"

"We've been over that a hundred times, my dear, since your darling mother left this world ten long years ago. Call it a monument. Call it legacy. Breakneck Gap is whatever any man wants to make of it. A haven, a refuge, a place to idle away time and contemplate great events. This is my K.G., my K.B.E. The living testament of Capt. William Weatherby, instead of a garter and a Sir before my name."

"You could have had it, you know, Daddy."

"Eh what? What's that?"

"Knight of the Garter, Knight of the British Empire. Admiral Sir William Weatherby, Tenth Earl of Leicestershire or wherever."

Weatherby laughed patronizingly and patted his swollen paunch. "How's that, silly girl?"

"You had influence, Daddy, both in the Admiralty and at Court. It was you who turned your back on all that. Daddy, to use an old Anglo-Saxon word recently dredged up by our American friends, you fucked it up."

Shock registered on Weatherby's face. "Marilee, I'm surprised at you! Such language. Such an odd idea in the first place. Circumstances conspired to force me to strike out in new fields of endeavor."

"With you and your fellow contrabandists as the chief conspirators," Marilee Weatherby handed back tartly.

"An officer of the Royal Navy must always look for opportunities to feather his nest," the deserter and former officer offered defensively.

"Oh, never mind, Daddy. I love you all the same. I think I have always loved you."

A strange light came to Weatherby's eyes. He felt a tightness in his chest and a stirring in his loins. "Is Daddy's little girl interested in showing that love in our special way right now?" he asked in a strained voice.

Musical laughter tinkled from Marilee's sweet lips. "Oh, Daddy, I thought you would never ask."

Separated from the cavalry units by unforeseen circumstances, this reporter fell into the hands of heathen Sioux savages, whose intentions were unknown . . .

Bound to a tree, Rachel sat and watched while the painted warriors stripped her horse of valuables. They made much of her spare supply of undergarments and the few cosmetics she carried along. One of them came to her, extending a small pot of rouge.

"Is this warpaint?" he asked in Lakota, gesturing toward her with the creamy matter.

"What? Huh? I don't understand. But I want to be your friend. You understand friend?"

"*Hiye haya*," the warrior uttered in confusion. The words meant nothing.

"That's right—friend. *Friend.*"

"Whren?"

"Yes, yes. I—I can do many things for you." All the while Rachel strained to invent ideas that she might be able to convey.

The other Sioux joined his companion. They spoke together in low tones, glancing often at the captive against the tree. At last, one bent and undid the rawhide rope. He stood Rachel up and began to remove her clothes.

"Say now, this is all a bit premature, isn't it? I mean, I hardly know you fellows. Ummm. Really, I don't think we should be—"

They had her naked now. Rachel shivered, a reaction of mixed fright and expectation. She noted the growing bulges behind the two loin cloths. Tentatively, as though shy of touching such light skin and pale, golden hair, the braves reached out and began to fondle her. Despite her perilous situation, Rachel found herself becoming aroused.

One warrior concentrated on the perfect halfmoon

mounds of her breasts, while the other stroked her belly and worked lower, to entangle his fingers in her fluffy thatch of pubic hair. With a wild cry of elation, this one jerked aside his pliable elkskin garment and revealed a truly wondrous organ.

Not so large as Eli Holten's, Rachel noted as she reached out to touch the swaying phallus. But it would do in a pinch. Like a playful child, the other Sioux threw her to the ground so his companion could have his way.

He entered her quickly and roughly. Rachel entwined her arms and legs around him as she thrilled to the thick, rigid object that plunged in and out of her slick passage. Her heart began to palpitate in rhythm with the shiveringly pleasant strokes. Expertly, she started to contract and relax, squeezing the churning shaft in a manner that brought a grunt of surprise and wide grin of appreciation to the sweating savage who lay atop her. His mouth went to one of her breasts, and bright lights burst in Rachel's head.

Using the tools of stone age savages, in ways that cannot be described in detail in a family newspaper, the powerful Sioux warriors tested this reporter's strength and courage . . .

Rachel went on composing while she labored in the sun to bring satisfaction to the muscular bronze-skinned man who shoved himself against her, causing goosebumps of delight to ripple across her skin. So they wanted to make love with her. Rachel found that entirely delightful. She'd show them some things they probably never got from their wives. In so doing, she reasoned, she stood a better chance of staying alive. She released her hold with one hand and beckoned the other brave to come closer.

Adroitly, she pantomined the position she wanted

him to take; legs alongside her head, knees against her shoulders. Then she whisked aside his breech cloth and pulled his throbbing penis close to her lips.

Smoothly she engulfed him and began her arduous work.

"Aaaah!" the warrior cried in pleased surprise. *"Ceazin! Ceazin!"*

After some twenty minutes of energetic effort on her part and his, the plunging, driving warrior cried out in ecstasy and climaxed prodigiously. Then he changed places with his companion.

Rachel squealed with delight as this new partner slathered his thick, stubby penis about in the free-flowing juices that soaked her burning cleft. She hungrily eyed the dripping organ above her face and reached up for it.

She had only closed her lips over its broad tip when a bolt of lightning shot through her as the other brave impaled her on his fat, fleshy lance. What a powerful accident to meet these two, she thought wildly as she warmed to newer and greater efforts. She would gladly keep this up all day.

Both warriors indulged in seconds before they and she felt sated. The trio lay in a heap for a long while, saying nothing. Then Rachel reached out, encircled a flaccid member with soft fingers and began to stroke it to life.

"Ceazin? Ceazin?" she inquired in a small, coaxing voice.

Later the Sans Arc braves walked a short distance away for a serious conference.

"I say we should kill her now and leave the body here," Buffalo Fat declared forcefully. "A yellow scalp will make good decorations for my new warshirt."

"Why? After all, our brothers have been without a woman for as long as we have. We should take her back as a gesture of our generosity. After the way we all ran and so many of our warriors died in the Valley-Where-the-Sky-Fell, they can use a little cheering up."

"You speak wisely, Two Suns. We'll make ready now."

With sure movements, the braves hoisted Rachel to her feet. They covered her nakedness with some of her spare clothing and lifted her onto her horse. Without comment, Two Suns took the reins and swung atop his pony. With Buffalo Fat in the lead, they headed back to the camp of Kicking Elk.

As they rode, Rachel's mind worked ceaselessly to re-write reality into a moving story of frontier courage.

Having exhibited endurance beyond even that of the fierce Sioux, this reporter won the primitive tribesmen's respect and admiration. Proudly this reporter rode across the vast plains with these new-found friends, headed for an unknown destination . . .

Chapter 7

"I've made a complete circuit of the rim, Tony," Eli Holten told Capt. Anthony Pierce. "There is no way in or out, except for this one narrow trail. If they have lookouts posted, it could turn into a death trap for us."

"We're less than five hundred yards away from the gap now," the cavalry officer observed. "Can you reconnoitre the situation?"

"Yes, sir. I'll start on it right away."

Before the scout could put spurs to his Morgan, a flanker sang out urgently. "Riders comin' in from the southwest!"

In a moment they thundered close by, passed the slower cavalry and made a dash directly for the opening in the high, caldera-like ridge that isolated the valley. All wore floppy hats, shabby greatcoats, or linen dusters. Even at a short distance, their identity, age, or sex could not be determined. Holten thought he heard a thin, frantic voice cry, "Eli!" but he couldn't be certain. Two minutes after they had appeared, the galloping horses carried their riders into the passage.

"Well, there goes any chance for surprise," Captain Pierce noted with disappointment.

"If Mr. Holten had been more attentive to his duties,

perhaps we would have been able to detain those men and keep the advantage," Lieutenant Holland sneered.

"I'll remind you, Lieutenant, that I made the decision to have Eli scout ahead of the column and place troopers on the flanks and as a rear guard," Captain Pierce snapped. "It was *you* who selected the detail. Since an officer is responsible for everything his men do or fail to do, their deficiency falls entirely on you."

Holland's face flushed and clouded up. For a second, Holten thought he might cry. The young lieutenant settled for a scowl and a pout that looked ridiculous with his thin, New Englander's lips. Abruptly, the affronted officer turned his mount to the left and cantered back to his place at the head of D Company's files.

Eli shrugged and trotted off toward the narrow defile that gave access to Breakneck Gap.

When he entered the tight passageway, the scout halted and dismounted. With quiet movements. Holten proceeded into the cut. He looked about him and marveled at the power of nature. Carved over eons by the running water of a small stream, the miniature canyon bent and twisted sinuously, following the path of less resistant rock and soil. Great spires stood out here and there, and sweeping overhangs that threatened to fall on the unwary slanted inwards from above. A sort of awe descended on Eli Holten, somewhat like what many persons feel inside a great cathederal. Halfway through the labyrinth, the terrain took on a dramatic change.

Holten had encountered no sentries, and he had wondered why. The broken, pock-marked ground gave him some reason. Huge gouts of earth had been ripped up, as though from artillery fire. Here and there he found the bones of men and horses, along with partially consumed bodies and abandoned weapons. It gave the scout pause. No cannon he knew of could be aimed blindly and fired with such accuracy as to confine all its strikes within ten feet of the thready trail.

Around another turn, the canyon straightened out. He saw more evidence of shelling and, in the distance some two thousand yards away, the roofs and upper stories of the buildings of Breakneck Gap. Quickly Holten changed his approach route, working in close to one wall, hugging the shadows there as he led his mount forward. As he progressed, the scout saw more evidence of a recent battle. Enough so that, when he came within sight of the town, its lack of visible fortifications left him puzzled.

Wagons sat idle at the four entrance roads of the small community. They could reasonably be assumed to constitute some sort of mobile barricades, the scout considered. Other than that, Eli saw nothing of a martial nature. If indeed cannon of some sort had been used, these weapons were kept out of sight until needed. Where?

Holten's attention went to the tall, towerlike brick building at the center of the cruciform streets of Breakneck Gap. Over it flew, quite incongruously, a large ensign of the Royal Navy. What had they walked into? Only here, Eli observed, behind the crenellations of the rooftop, did he see anyone walking guard post.

Two men shared this onerous task. They paced listlessly, stopping frequently to peer downward at a crowd gathered around the riders who had by that time reached the small village. Other than word of the cavalry's approach, what else had generated such excitement? Holten eased through the tall grass to get a

72

better look.

Twenty minutes passed while the scout examined all sides of the bustling community. He learned nothing more about its defenses and decided to return to the column.

Capt. William C. Weatherby roused himself and climbed from the bed. He looked down at the full, lush breasts of his partner and produced a winsome smile. How very nice it had been. As always, of course. Only this time with a special, piquant flavor of excitement rarely engendered between two people. He couldn't understand lesser men's attitudes toward women.

Mere sex objects? Something to use, abuse, and throw aside? Hardly. He had dearly cherished every woman in his life, even those with whom he had not shared an amorous attachment. Bloody damned barbarians!

As he quickly dressed, he considered the fate in store, at the hands of such men, for these white women Mullins was supposed to be bringing in. Would they consider them any more than the semihuman redskin females they now used to disport themselves? Only moments before, the sentry atop the magazine had called out that riders approached. From the number, it had to be Mullins. He would have to hurry.

At the mirror, Weatherby fastened the last gold buttons of his coat and adjusted the hang of his sword. He turned back to the lovely vision on the bed and his voice came out warm with fondness.

"Quite magnificent, my dear. Your talent grows with every day. Now, I must go attend to important matters. Until later, my love?"

Downstairs, the lord and master of Breakneck Gap

stalked across the large "bullpen" and out onto the porch. By the time he arrived, Freddy Mullins and his captives waited on horseback in the dusty street.

"Good to have you back, Mister Mullins. Were you successful in your mission?"

"Aye-aye, sir. Me an' the boys had to abandon the wagons, though, and bring the women in on horseback, because the army is headed this way."

"The army, is it?"

"Aye. About two companies."

"My, my. How stimulating. Well, set down your charges. Boatswain, pass the word for Mister Yardley. My compliments, and have him start preparing the defenses. We're about to be paid a visit by the Americans."

"Aye-aye, sir."

Under Freddy's direction, the men with him pulled the Sioux girls and the soiled doves of the Thunder Saloon from their mounts and arranged them in a line. Not one to be hurried by anything, up to and including the Second Coming, Captain Weatherby set about minutely inspecting each of the new recruits for his prison brothels. As he progressed down the line, little Elizabeth Brewster forced herself to step forward.

She cast an anxious glance at this man who was so obviously in command. He would understand, she thought in her heart of hearts. He simply *had* to. She gave him her purest, most innocent little-girl look.

Weatherby's eyes glowed when he noticed her. "Aha! What have we here?"

"Oh, please, sir. You must listen to me. I'm Elizabeth Brewster. My father is Harlan Wellington Brewster. He is a federal judge. I should not be here with these— these— *harlots*. I am not one of them. My family is on its

74

way to California, where my father will take the bench in the Federal District Court in San Francisco. We only stopped off until my oldest brother could be mustered out of the army."

"Well now, that is quite interesting. How is it that you are with these other, ah, ladies?"

"An accident. Your men abducted me off the street outside the Thunder Saloon. Now, I can understand why a gentleman like yourself would send for drabs such as these and red squaws to sate the urges of the riff-raff you employ. That is in the way of things. But I am pure, sir. That is to say, I am a virgin and am to remain unsullied until the day of my marriage. Please arrange to have me escorted back to Eagle Pass, sir."

"Uh-hemmm. Odd situation, indeed. You say your father is a judge?" Elizabeth nodded. "This is a severe breach of regulations, Mister Mullins. I find it most unsettling. Do you know the men responsible for this terrible mistake?"

"Aye, sir. Clem and Dorkus."

"Very well. Perhaps twenty stripes will sharpen their thinking in future. This is barbaric. Unforgivable." He bent low to bring his face on a level with the strikingly beautiful little girl. "I can't tell you how sorry I am that this misfortune had befallen you, my dear. I will arrange accommodations for you, and see you have an opportunity to recover yourself before beginning the return journey to Eagle Pass." He came erect and stood with hands behind his back while he addressed those assembled around the new arrivals.

"Mister Tandy. See to the young lady, if you please. Take her to a secure place where she might freshen up. Also see that she is provided with refreshment and food.

Now, the rest of you. Hear this. If I learn of any man who has molested, or attempts in future to molest, this dear young lady, I shall personally haul on the lanyard when you are hoisted to the yardarm."

"Oh, thank you, sir. Thank you most kindly. I—I was certain that a fine gentleman like yourself would take pity on my plight and render assistance."

Weatherby bowed low and took her hand. He pressed it momentarily to his lips and righted his posture. "Your humble servant, Miss Brewster. Now, you must excuse me. Pressing matters demand my immediate attention. Young Mister Tandy here will see to your needs."

"Forward . . . at the trot . . . ho!" Lieutenant Holland echoed the command with gusto.

My God, Eli Holten thought. Holland's taking this thing almost as seriously as Georgie Custer and his Seventh.

Now formed four abreast, the officers and men of the two cavalry companies advanced down the sloping side of the valley toward the distant buildings of Breakneck Gap. It still bothered Holten that he had no idea what purpose the tall brick tower served. A hotel, two saloons, and three bordellos comprised the remaining part of town. Why the tower? And why the short mast, spars and rigging atop it? As they drew nearer, a series of what appeared to be small black balls ran up one thin line, then bloomed into colorful pennants. On a second halyard, the huge blood-red flag with a blue cross and white outlining still waved lazily in the breeze.

"That's a British flag," Captain Pierce declared in surprise. "I thought they'd learned their lesson in 1814."

"I saw it earlier and neglected to tell you, Tony. I wonder what they have in mind?"

"I don't think we're dealing with an invasion," the captain returned dryly. "Whoever is responsible for this has to be on his own."

"And a few bricks shy of a load," the scout added.

"Considering those naval signal flags, I'd take it that he didn't have both oars in the water," the erudite officer responded. "It bothered me when you reported evidence of artillery fire, Eli. When I saw it myself, I grew more concerned. Worse is your statement that you saw no indication of any cannon in the town. Where are they? I think we'll halt here and ride forward with a small party to parlay."

"Good idea, Tony. Just because I didn't see any big guns doesn't mean they aren't there. That'll give us a chance to look things over at a close range without exciting an immediate retaliation."

"Fancy words, for you," Captain Pierce observed. He commanded the troops to halt and turned in his saddle. "Lieutenant Dill, Sergeant McInnes, front and center. You will accompany Mr. Holten and myself to parlay with whoever runs this town."

Three men awaited them as the four representatives of the Army cantered forward. When the quartet reached a point some fifty yards away, Eli realized that the one in the center wore some sort of uniform. White trousers, a blue coat with a lot of gold trim, and a cocked hat.

"Looks like the limey navy," Sergeant McInnes remarked in a mutter.

At twenty feet's distance, Captain Pierce halted the party. He silently studied the trio in front of him before

77

making comment.

"Good afternoon. I am Capt. Anthony Pierce of the Twelfth U. S. cavalry. Is one of you gentlemen the mayor of this, ah, town?"

Weatherby took a step forward. "A good afternoon to you, sir. I am commanding this expedition. Captain The Honorable William Weatherby at your service," he declared, settling only a minor title on himself.

"It is my duty to inform you, Captain, that your little community is in direct violation of the Red Cloud treaty. White settlement in the Black Hills is expressly forbidden."

"Oh, come now, Captain," Weatherby blustered. "What about Deadwood? For that matter, of what value is a treaty concluded with a savage? You can not hold back the tide of Destiny. It is the white man's lot to populate this vast continent from sea to sea. The whim of a few bloody natives shouldn't stand in the way. D'you think we would have done so well in India if we'd let Mister Wog dictate terms to us?"

"This is not the British Empire, and the Dakota Territory is not India. I see you've erected barricades," Pierce went on, changing the subject. "They will have to be withdrawn so we might enter and make an inventory, prior to your removal."

"I dare say, there'll be no such thing as a, ah, 'removal.' Whatever possessed you to believe you could come in here and uproot us like this?"

"The Sioux have it that this is particularly sacred soil this year. They are on the move already. The Sun Dance is to be held here. Before then, you and your people have to be gone from here, and the buildings demolished."

"Never, sir! It is the Army's responsibility to insure the safety of white men, is it not?"

"It is also the Army's responsibility to enforce the terms of the treaty. This is Sioux land. You are here illegally. If you do not vacate this property, on which you are squatting in violation of the treaty, the Army will be obliged to move you. By force if necessary."

Weatherby's eyes narrowed. "By gad, sir! Are you threatening an officer of His Majesty's Navy?"

"Somehow I get the feeling it's been a long time since you've served the British Empire. Shall we say, perhaps, that you might even find it, ah, embarrassing to be returned to the jurisdiction of the Crown?"

"Now see here, you upstart popinjay!" Weatherby blustered. "Possession is nine-tenths of the law. We are here, we intend to stay, and we are prepared to defend our intentions if required."

"I regret to say that you leave us no choice." Pierce raised his voice so he could be heard by the men gathered behind the dirt-filled wagons that formed the barricade. "This is your last opportunity. Open that barrier and make ready to leave with us peacefully, or suffer the consequences."

"Begone, sir! We have nothing else to say to each other, save that you have made a most grievous error, sir. One for which the men under your command will pay most sanguinarily."

Abruptly, Weatherby turned on his heel and marched smartly back inside the town.

"Let's return to the troops," Captain Pierce instructed quietly. "We will attack immediately."

These magnificent horsemen of the plains took this reporter to their main encampment, where scores of their fellows waited. Would it be war? Would the tenuously held peace continue? Everything hinged upon the proper actions of the brave soldiers of the Twelfth Cavalry, and the skill of the Chief Scout, Eli Holten. When our small caravan arrived in the Sioux encampment —

"Ouch!" Rachel cried out as Stone Heart unceremoniously dragged her from her horse and threw her at the feet of a tall, brawny redman, who glowered down at her with pure contempt written in the craggy lines of his face.

Or at least what she could see of his face, Rachel amended quickly, hidden behind all that warpaint. She swallowed heavily and batted her eyes at him. Immediately the warriors crowded around, yelling excitedly.

"*Uśi maya ye!*" Stone Heart bellowed. His command for attention immediately silenced those nearest the center of interest. "We give this woman to Kicking Elk for his pleasure and as a slave," the trusted lieutenant went on in Lakota. "There are many of the white women to take for our enjoyment. This is but the first. We shall have many more!"

"*Hau! Hau!*" the braves cried back.

"I thank you for this gift, though I have no need of it," Kicking Elk replied. "Soon we shall be within the *tacante canku*, the heart-shaped path. Once we are inside the spiritual hoop that encircles our holy Black Hills, all must be done in a sacred manner. For now, though, I shall take this insignificant one to my lodge."

Kicking Elk bent and drew Rachel to her knees by pulling her hair. She made a face and tried to twist away, only to be kicked playfully in the belly.

"Tell me of what you have seen, Stone Heart."

"The pony-soldiers ride toward the Valley-Where-the-Sky-Fell. Many of them. They do not bring the long guns that shoot far away. With them rides Tall Bear of the Oglala."

"Then truly the seeker of yellow metal must have reached the soldiers. They have given serious thought to our message."

"This is so, Kicking Elk. Even now they go to round up the trespassers at the sacred valley."

"That is good." Kicking Elk looked down at Rachel, whose attention had become riveted on the bulge behind his loin cloth. "I go now to teach manners to this one."

Inside the low skin lodge of the war chief, Rachel needed no prompting to remove her clothing. Kicking Elk jerked aside his breech cloth and revealed a marvelous endowment, compared with those of his subordinates. Eagerly the young reporter reached for it.

Rachel cooed softly with anticipatory delight as she wrapped strong fingers around the throbbing shaft that swayed upward from Kicking Elk's groin. She went to her knees and crawled close to him. With an eager flick of her tongue she licked the bulging sack that hung below the manly-scented lance, then thrust it boldly into her open, hungry mouth.

Kicking Elk looked down on her endeavors and grunted his appreciation of this special attention. He sighed contentedly as Rachel began to work the length of his manhood deeper into her warm, moist orifice. What he had intended to start as nothing more than a degradation of this white captive was rapidly turning into something quite delightful.

This reporter's escort presented him to the leader of the large warparty. We found instant rapport, although at the insistence of

81

the other fighting men, the most harrowing of tests had to be endured before your correspondent had an opportunity to engage in a delightful meal that sustained both body and spirit. Never has this traveling journalist been treated to such open-hearted hospitality.

Rachel turned the phrases over in her head as she worked to take in even more of the powerful warrior's most important part. Oh, my, would she ever have some things to tell Eli Holten when she got away from here!

Chapter 8

Two lines of cavalry, drawn up in company front formation, waited atop their snorting mounts. Ahead of them, sabres flashing in the sun, their officers made ready.

"Pre-pare to draw carbines . . . ." Captain Pierce called out. "Draw . . . carbines!"

A scrape of leather and a rattle of saddle rings followed.

Tension harshened Anthony Pierce's voice as he gave the next command. "Bugler . . . sound the charge!"

A staccato of brassy notes pealed across the valley.

Before the last bar had been played, the thunder of pounding hoofs rolled ominously toward the men behind the barricades. Swelling like inflating balloons, the blue tide grew larger as the tightly aligned files neared the town. Several inmates of the brothels appeared on their balconies, and Marilee Weatherby took a place near the center of activity, not far from where her father stood in command of his forces. Unbidden, the troopers began to shout in bloodlust.

"Yeeee-aaaaah-hooo!" From several throats came the eerie wail of the Rebel yell.

"First file, prepare to fire!" Pierce shouted, well aware

that the men could not hear him. "By volley . . . FIRE!" he shouted as he swung down his extended sabre.

Forty-three Springfield .45-70 carbines snarled retribution at the criminal element of Breakneck Gap.

The heavy slugs smashed into the loaded wagons. Hot lead sent splinters and gouts of dirt flying upward. The tremendous impact jarred the men sheltered behind them. With a remarkable show of discipline, the defenders held their fire.

"Second file . . . prepare to fire!" Pierce commanded. "By volley . . . FIRE!"

This time the bullets cracked past barely over the tops of the makeshift barricades. They riddled the building fronts and a few moaned off forlornly from the rounded brick edifice of the magazine. Some of the bawds shrilled in fright and disappeared inside to imagined safety. Marilee jittered with excitement, her nipples hardening and her secret parts moistening in response to the heady aroma of burnt powder.

Less than three hundred yards separated the charging cavalry from the small community of Breakneck Gap. Holten noticed it first, then Pierce pointed to their right, where two highly polished artillery pieces had appeared from large double doors in the brick tower. They had expected something like this, and it had served as the signal for Pierce to turn away his command.

Too late, as the fat Whitney's, with their hexagonal bored tubes, swung into place. Immediately, the assistant gunners banged against one of the brass balls of the inertial breech openers with heavy wooden mallets. The screws spun, and the crews leaped to swing the threaded breechblocks open. Twelve-pound projectiles of case shot slid up the 2.75 inch bores, followed by silk bags containing one and three-quarters pounds of powder. Then the breeches swung closed. Once more the assistant gunners banged against the nearest brass ball of the inertial devices.

Captain Weatherby's dress sword cut a silvery arc through the air. The thousand-pound guns reared backward at the detonation of the charges, and the long, slender projectiles sped up the hundred-four-inch barrels.

Although less effective than case or canister shot from a twelve-pounder Napoleon or a three-inch-bore mountain howitzer, the shards of metal from the exploding shells ripped and tore into the ranks of troopers. Horses shrieked and reared, men wailed in pain or terror. Many fell from their saddles, not all of them wounded. The orderly attack turned instantly into an insane melee.

"Sound recall! Sound recall, for God's sake!" Lieutenant Holland howled in mindless horror.

Before Captain Pierce could give the order to retreat, fully one third of his command fell to the rapidfire slaughter of Weatherby's Whitworths. More than three-quarters of those lay dead amid the welter of blood and entrails of their butchered horses.

"Back! Get back!" Pierce shouted as the bugler began the first notes of recall.

"Turn back, man!" he bellowed in the ear of a white-faced, glazed-eyed private who continued to charge directly into the depressed muzzle of one breech-loading cannon.

A great orange ball formed at the black opening. A crimson-slashed billow of smoke followed it. A moment later, the shell, traveling at fifteen hundred feet per second, struck the battle-hypnotized trooper in the abdomen.

He came apart like a squashed strawberry.

Blood, bone, and intestines flew in every direction as the case shot projectile exploded. His horse screamed piteously and crumpled in a gory heap, shredded by some twenty shell fragments. A moment later, the second Whitworth opened fire again.

The shot landed directly between the churning legs of Captain Pierce's horse. It seemed to leap into the air, long, purple-gray strands of intestine stringing out of its ripped belly. Both legs shattered by case shrapnel, the stalwart officer flopped on its back in helpless agony. Another hideous whinny and a final bound into the air sent the foam-flecked bay to the ground. Its heavy body rolled over onto the injured officer amid a sound of snapping bones.

Eli Holten saw what happened and cut across the murderous curtain of fire from the enemy to reach his friend's side. It took superhuman effort on his part and that of Sergeant McInnes and a benumbed trooper to lift the dead horse and drag Captain Pierce free. His chest had an oddly flat, bulged out appearance.

That alone told Eli what terrible internal injuries could be expected. Gently he lifted Pierce and eased him astride a nervous mount. He recovered the reins of his Morgan and swung into the saddle. With Sergeant McInnes' assistance, he held Pierce upright as they galloped away from certain death.

From her place on a balcony near the battlements, Marilee Weatherby watched with fascination. These were real, well-trained troops. Yet they had scattered like frightened quail. How brilliant her father had been in choosing the fast-loading Whitworth guns to defend Breakneck Gap! She saw the officer leading the soldiers fall to a burst of case shot. Then her heart quickened, and she thrilled to the daring sight of a buckskin-clad man racing to the injured captain's rescue. She couldn't help but admire the brave act she witnessed, and she silently wished the victim and his savior good luck.

How romantic and exciting to see such heroism as that exhibited before her, as the apparent civilian braved withering fire to save his comrade! Too bad he'd probably die soon also.

"Keep going!" Eli shouted to the confused, demoralized troops. "All the way back into the gap!"

"No. No! We've got to regroup and charge again!" Lieutenant Holland countermanded. Seized by a strange dementia, he had forgotten his former terror. He desired only to wreak slaughter on those who had butchered his first field command.

"Don't be a fool, Lieutenant. Those cannon will cut us to pieces," Holten told him.

"I'm in command now, goddammit!" Holland shrieked in near hysteria. "It's our duty to attack and attack and attack until the enemy is defeated. Sergeant, rally the men."

"As you say, *sir*," McInnes replied in a tone that made clear his opinion of such orders.

Many of the troopers had strung out far ahead of the cluster of officers and men around Eli Holten. McInnes bellowed at them to turn around, only to have his voice drowned out in the crash of exploding shells. No matter their distance, the deadly Whitworths continued to rain destruction and death among the frightened cavalrymen.

"Regroup! Regroup! Form on me!" Lieutenant Holland shouted in a breaking voice.

Slowly, as they shook off their initial shock and fear, the men began to comply.

"What about the captain, Lieutenant Holland?" McInnes inquired.

"He's wounded. Probably done for. Leave him here."

"Alone?"

"Hell yes, alone, Sergeant. Now do as you are told. Form these men up for another charge."

"Beggin' the Lieutenant's pardon, sir . . ."

"You do not have my pardon, Sergeant. Follow your orders or I'll have you shot."

"Before or after those fuckin' cannon have done with me, sir?"

"Insubordination!" Holland squeaked in beet-faced fury. "We'll take this up after the fight."

"If either of us is alive, sir."

"That's defeatist talk, Sergeant."

"Yes, sir. As you say, sir." McInnes turned in his saddle. "Over here, men. Form up on the lieutenant. We're goin' back an' teach them spalpeen bastards a lesson!"

"You three men," Eli Holten's deep, angry voice broke through the sound of bursting shells and excited talk of the troopers. "Stay with Captian Pierce."

"No, they won't!" Holland screamed. "I'll not have my decisions disputed."

"Do it," Holten snapped back as he turned his level, gray gaze on the young officer. Their bleak appearance had the deadly menace of an iceberg.

Holland blinked and turned away. "Make ready, men!" he shouted in a suddenly unsteady voice.

Charges burst among the terrified horses and claimed

more lives, even as Lieutenant Holland gave the command to charge. Within the first three hundred yards of the dash, a quarter of his remaining force fell from their saddles. A moaning bit of metal ripped the hat from Holland's head, and another severed his mount's left ear. Reluctantly, while still out of rifle range, he ordered the sounding of recall.

Marilee Weatherby jumped up and down and clapped her small hands as she watched the courageous soldiers return to test her father's defenses once more. How noble and dedicated they were. The sharp cracks of the Whitworths kept up a steady rhythm, and blue-uniformed figures flew form the backs of their mounts. On they came. Ah, Marilee thought, in the fine tradition of the stalwart British horse regiments. Why, this was almost like that famous battle at Balaclava.

" 'Honor the Light Brigade,' " Marilee quoted sketchily. " 'O! What a charge they made. While cannon volleyed and thundered, into the valley of death rode the six hundred.' " Tears of pride and patriotism filled her eyes.

But these are not British soldiers, she told herself angrily. They are Americans and they want to throw us out of our haven. Her jaw hardened into a grimly determined set and she looked with glowing eyes to where her beloved father sweated and roared orders amid the powder-grimed men manning the barricades.

Rachel Johnson slept peacefully on Kicking Elk's chest. She breathed softly, a contented smile on her lips. The great warrior stoically stared heavenward, although his big left hand gently stroked the white woman's blond hair. His dream had not told him of this one. How did her coming affect what they had to do? Would all-out war come with the whites? If so, after using this woman, he would have to enter the *initi* for the renewing ceremony. For many hours of purification in the sweat lodge, he thought ruefully as he felt himself stiffening once more with urgent desire for her creamy white body.

Faced with a deep moral dilemma, Kicking Elk pondered his situation as his reddened manhood climbed from his belly. He had come to kill whites. This one as well, if she persisted in entering the sacred circle of the Black Hills. Yet the golden-haired one had found a place in his heart.

Since early in the day they had made love in his lodge. He had thought to rape her, only to find her more than willing. She seemed never to tire of the tender combat. Even now, in her sleep, her soft fingers gently squeezed his pulsing shaft as it grew more rigid. What could he do? It would be madness to take her back with him. She would be impossible to train to camp work. Yet he could not bring himself to pull the knife from the bullhide sheath in the heap of their clothing at his side and slice it across her throat.

He couldn't, truth to tell, even delegate the task to one of his followers. She seemed to love — life too well for that. Would the pony-soldiers be successful in driving out the whites who profaned the sacred ground of the Sun Dance? Did they even care? Words! Funny black marks on a sheet of paper, he thought scornfully. That is all a treaty meant to the whites. They broke them even before the writing liquid dried on the scrolls they gave to the treaty chiefs. He would wait, though. He had given his word.

These reflections in his troubled heart were interrupted by the faint sound of distant thunder. Kicking Elk's keen hearing soon let him recognize the ominous rumbles as something far more sinister than the anger of nature.

"Whitworth guns," Captain Pierce gasped out as a degree of consciousness returned to him.

He lay on a blanket under the shelter of a large pine, outside the narrow defile that led to Breakneck Gap. Lieutenant Edward Holland knelt on one side, looking like nothing so much as a frightened, confused little boy. Opposite him, Eli Holten hunkered down on his heels and peered intently at the waxen, yellow-green hue of the severely wounded officer's face. Eli felt a tightness in his chest. His friend would die soon. Gingerly, the lieutenant dabbed a damp cloth at his commander's oily, sweat-sheened forehead.

The devastation of the second attack had quickly drained Holland of his momentary surge of bravado. He had ordered the retreat and quickly took his place at the head of the fleeing column. Bent low to his horse's neck, he had whimpered as they galloped away. The deadly accurate fire of the Whitworths had kept pace with them fully halfway through the gap. Men and animals had died horribly, and the haunting memory of those ferocious guns remained with every one of the survivors.

"What are those?" Holten inquired, his face creased with worry for his old friend.

"That's what Weatherby has in Breakneck Gap."

"I've never heard of them. From what part of Hell did they come?"

"They're of English origin. Came into use about '63. B-both sides had them in the war. They load from the breech. The one—ones he has are big, the tw-twelve-pounders. They fire a long, thin projectile, propelled by a one-point-seven-five-pound charge. The riflings are made in a hexagonal design. Th-they have spec-spectacular range and accuracy. Because of the slender shape of the shells, they carry only a small bursting charge. Rapid fire and long range make up for that. Most were mounted on ships. Others, like these, had been outfitted with artillery carriages. They can hit targets accurately at twenty-eight hundred yards—nearly two miles."

"That's why they pounded us even after we were out of sight in the canyon," Eli responded. "But how did Weatherby get them?"

"Easy enough." A thin, slick film of red formed and oozed over the captain's lips. He coughed and his face crumpled in pain as he made a feeble grab at his aching chest. "Weatherby was once in the Royal Navy. He could have stolen them when he deserted."

"He never said he had deserted," Lieutenant Holland countered.

"You can be sure he did, or he wouldn't be here, consorting with criminals. Listen close, Eli. There—there's not m-much time. No one can take that place. N-not with what we have to counter those Whitworths with. If man could—could on-only fly. Come up over the ridge and drop explosive shells on their heads."

Raving, the scout thought. Completely out of his mind in pain. Man flying and delivering explosives from the sky. Pierce hadn't long, and Holten knew it. He placed a canteen to the officer's lips.

"Take it easy, Tony. We'll get a wagon here for you."

A harsh, grating sound that might have been a cynical laugh came raw from Pierce's throat. "You mean for my corpse, don't you? I know I'm dying. An—and I know it is impossible to take Breakneck Gap by conventional means. B-but I—I want you to promise me something."

"Sure, Tony. What is it?"

"I wan-want you to p-promise me . . . that . . . you will try. Please, Eli. Say you'll at least try."

"I—" Eli found he could not lie to the dying soldier. "I'm afraid I can't, Tony. You see, I believe in how invincible Breakneck Gap is, too. If we had the time, we could dynamite closed the trail through that canyon and starve them out."

"The . . . Sioux . . . won't . . . let you." Pierce's voice had become only a frail thread of whisper.

Shame burned in the scout's breast. "I know, Tony. I've never walked away from a fight before. Only, how . . . ?"

"B-by deceit," Anthony Pierce gasped out in the last moment before he vomited up a mighty spew of black blood and, quivering in release, died.

Chapter 9

He paused nervously outside the door, somewhat like a young swain making his first courting call. Irritably he ran a thick finger around a stiff collar of his shirt, then removed his large cocked hat and rapped lightly on the door.

"Wh-who is it?"

"Captain Weatherby, Miss Brewster. Are you, ah, able to receive visitors?"

"Oh! Oh, yes. Please do come in."

Weatherby entered and bowed low. "Your servant, Miss Brewster. I wondered if you would enjoy partaking of tea? I can have it sent up straight away. Cook's prepared some lovely cakes, and there's lemon and cream if you wish."

He found himself babbling and stopped abruptly.

"Why, that would be delightful," Elizabeth replied, enjoying the role of the honored guest. "Won't you please sit down?"

"A moment, my dear. Let me summon our repast."

Weatherby went to the door and opened it. "Mr. Tandy," he bellowed down the hall. "Have Cook send up the tea service. And an assortment of pastries, if you please."

"Aye-aye, sir."

Weatherby returned to the center of the room and settled his comfortable girth in a brocaded loveseat. Then he gazed earnestly at his young captive. After a moment's silence, he sighed heavily and rubbed his hands together.

"Now, as to your return to your people. I'm afraid there will be a slight delay. There is a state of hostility between the United States and us. I'm sure you heard the firing earlier?"

Elizabeth nodded, her eyes wide, expression solemn. She started to make a comment, but the former naval officer rushed on.

"Soldiers of the United States Army attempted to force us out of our rightful property here in the valley. We resisted. So it may be some while before we reach some sort of suitable compromise agreement and be able to send you off to Eagle Pass. I hope you understand."

"I — I'm not sure, Captain Weatherby. Isn't this — the, ah, valley, a part of the United States?"

"A mere formality, my dear Miss Brewster," Weatherby dismissed it with a wave of his hand. "Land belongs to those who hold it. But that's a complicated legal affair far too complex for your pretty head. Has Tandy treated you well?" he changed the subject.

"Oh, yes. He's really a sweet little boy," Elizabeth responded.

You should see him when he's had a few tots of rum and his pecker's as stiff as a marlin spike, Weatherby thought, amused. His verbal reply was considerably more moderate.

"Humm. I suppose from your, er, superior years, he

95

would seem merely a child. He's thirteen, you know."

Elizabeth laughed delightedly for the first time since she had paused outside the Thunder Saloon. "You're teasing me, Captain."

Weatherby joined her merriment. "Yes, I am. You, ah, remind me of my daughter when she was younger."

"Is she far from you?"

"No. As a matter of fact, she's right here. Been at my side, fair weather or foul, since her dear mother died ten years ago. She'll reach her majority two months from now."

"Is she betrothed?"

"Certainly not!" Weatherby seemed to bristle at this suggestion. He took a deep breath and went on. "I do hope you two shall be friends during your stay."

"Oh, I will try to make it so," Elizabeth responded sincerely.

A knock sounded at the door. "Ah, here's our tea," Weatherby announced as he rose and crossed the room. He spoke commandingly to the small, slim boy as the lad entered with a silver tray that held a tea service and a plate of cakes.

"Mr. Tandy, would you stay and serve us, please?"

"Aye-aye, sir." Geoffrey Tandy grinned impishly at Elizabeth as she set his burden down on a small, rosewood table.

He smelled of rum, Elizabeth thought as he came close and handed her a cup and saucer. And, she noted, he had an interestingly large bulge in his tight, white trousers. Whatever could cause that? Was he deformed in some manner? she wondered.

Low fires crackled in a dozen stone rings as the surviving members of the Twelfth Cavalry patrol prepared their evening meal. Eli Holten sat alone, staring stonily off in the direction of Breakneck Gap. There was nowhere in the valley, from the ridge crest to the floor, that could not be covered by the withering fire of those damned Whitworth guns. Use deceit, his dying friend had told him.

Well, Tony Pierce lay under a shallow pile of dirt and stones, waiting the time when he and the other dead could be recovered and returned to Fort Rawlins for a formal burial ceremony. He had not lived long enough to enlarge on his idea. For the time being, Holten had not the least insight as to what it might mean. He stretched and rose to cross over to the nearest fire for some coffee.

A small wooden box, with a five-pound bag of beans inside, sat beside the corporal detailed to attend this mess fire. The familiar "flying angel" trademark on the carton identified it to Holten as Arbuckle's premium grade. The heady aroma of the boiling brew filled his nostrils. He bent and poured a measure into his tin cup.

"It ain't no good if the spoon don't stand up in it," the young corporal told him goodnaturedly.

"You've got that right, corporal," Eli replied with a grin.

Alone again, Eli sipped and thought. For the first time, nothing enlightening came to him. Approaching footsteps, crunching through the brittle grass, brought him out of his dark reverie.

"What do we do now, Mister Holten?"

Eli looked up at the troubled face of Lieutenant Holland. "That's not for me to say. You're in command now."

"I . . . uh . . . that is, *technically* I am. Only I don't want to be."

"Why's that?"

"It's—well, after what happened this afternoon, I don't feel qualified, or competent, to command two companies. Or what's left of them," he added with chagrin.

"Mr. Holland, if you hadn't been considered qualified, the Army would never have sent you here. As to competent, that's a matter for your superiors to decide. The fact remains that you are the senior Army officer present, and you are in command."

"But, sir—I mean, you do outrank me," Holland protested, his voice breaking. "At least as far as the paperwork goes. You should be the one to take over."

"I am a civilian, Mister Holland."

"Yes. And the only one here who knows what to do. How to get these men safely out of here."

"Where would you propose to go, Mr. Holland?"

"Why—uh, to lay some sort of siege on Breakneck Gap. A messenger should be sent to Fort Rawlins, reporting what has happened, the tactical situation, and requesting reinforcements. Then we close off that single way in and starve those sons of bitches out of there."

"And I'll be happy to be that messenger. That's *my* job. *Yours* is to command this patrol. For my own part, I think we should all go back to Fort Rawlins. There isn't time for a siege. Those Sioux won't wait. If we want to keep the peace, we have to drive Weatherby and his people out of there before the rest of the Sioux Nation arrives here for the Sun Dance."

"Wh-what do you propose, then, sir?"

"We come back with the entire regiment, if necessary,

the gallopers and even the heavy ordnance. Those twelve-pounders can do a lot of damage. Not at so long a range as the Whitworths, but overall they are more destructive. We can shell that town until it's nothing but a rubble heap."

"We could lose a lot of men that way."

"We could lose the whole damned territory if the Sioux take to the warpath."

Holland winced. "I see what you mean. It might be better to talk this all over with General Corrington and launch a larger offensive. Even so, we'd prefer if you took command, sir."

" '*We?*' "

"Yes, sir," came the voice of Lieutenant Dill out of the gathering darkness. "I'm junior by two years to Holland here. We talked it over, the officers and NCO's. We all think that it would be best."

"Sure an' that goes for me an' the boys, too," Sergeant McInnes chimed in as he walked up.

"You're all out of your minds," Eli Holten told them, though he couldn't stop the grin of pride as he felt the warm glow of their respect.

Grizzley Jack Ropon dug a pesky louse from behind his ear as he and a dozen men walked their horses along the narrow defile. What he and the boys had heard sounded good. Now it was time to find out if any truth lay behind it. The crudely cut, handmade leather hat sagged its brim so that it appeared Jack had no neck, only a misshapen lump atop his thick, sloping shoulders. With his free hand he searched out a short length of twist tobacco and bit off a respectable chew.

Long ago his snaggled teeth had been stained a permanent yellow-brown by the juice of his companionable weed. Coupled with a squint eye, they gave him a shifty, unsavory look. It went well with his occupation.

Jack and the cutthroats who rode with him made a specialty of leading unsuspecting homesteaders into the wilderness to rob and murder them. A lot less risky than robbing banks or stealing cattle, Jack had decided back in the booming expansion days of the Fifties. Why, most of them pilgrims didn't even know how to use a gun — even if they owned one. That had changed somewhat following the war.

Even so, the wide-eyed adventure seekers made easier targets than stagecoach guards and railroad agents. When he had heard word of a town that had driven off Sioux *and* the Army, he just knew he had to see it for himself.

When the baker's dozen of hardcases trotted over the remaining hundred yards to Breakneck Gap, three times as many rifles covered their progress. Armed sentries met them at the edge of town and escorted them to the front of the *Hart and Hound*, the smaller of the two saloons, where Captain Weatherby happened to be holding court at the time.

Dressed in his former finery, the commanding figure of Captain Weatherby strode out onto the porch to greet the new arrivals. "I am Capt. William C. Weatherby, late of the Royal Navy. This is my town. We have only two requirements of those who come here. You must have money to spend and the willingness to fight in the community's defense, if attacked."

"We have both," Grizzley Jack rumbled back.

"Then you are welcome. Rape is not tolerated, nor is

100

murder. For either you can be hanged, as you can for robbing anyone in the valley. Insubordination and riotous behavior are flogging offenses. Other than that there are no laws. Come in and sign the articles. The first drink is on me."

"What's these here 'articles?' " Jack asked suspiciously.

"Why, the ship's articles under which we operate and the crew is mustered. It makes you one of us for the duration of your stay."

"Seems I've heard somewhere that a ship's captain can flog a man or have him strung up under those sort of articles," one of Jack's companions muttered dubiously.

Weatherby uttered a snort of laughter. "Why, bless me, that's correct. We run a tight ship here. It has proven to be the best way."

"They say you ran off the Army," Jack challenged.

"We did, sir. Only two days ago. We effected nearly fifty percent casualties."

"What? With these few men? We heard it was near to two companies that rode in here."

"And barely more than one that escaped," Weatherby added. "Have you ever heard of a Whitworth?"

"Whazzat?"

"A cannon, my friend. A breech-loading, rifled-barrel artillery piece that can throw a projectile nearly two miles. We have two of them."

Jack whistled tunelessly. He was impressed and he could see that these calm remarks had moved his sidekicks also.

"We've been out, ah, robbin' here and there," Jack informed the imperious looking man before him. "We're tired, we're hungry, and we're sure as the devil horny.

Can you take care of those needs? Not necessarily in that order, mind."

"We certainly can. And more. What about a bath?"

"A *bath*?" Jack echoed. "Who ever takes one o' them?"

"Rest assured we do around here and," Weatherby paused to sniff, "you could certainly use one right now. Come in, sign up, and then go about your pleasures. Everything you could ever want is available in Breakneck Gap—for a price."

Amy Smith, nee Peters, lay on her back, feigning pleasure while a burly gunner with a thick Cockney accent rutted atop her. Because of their decisive routing of the cavalry troops, they had been given first go at the new additions to the bordellos. Although once, by inclination and choice, this had been her profession, she felt deeply humiliated by this sudden return to whoredom.

She was, after all, a married woman. Wife of a minister of the Gospel, and a leader in her community. She had found true marital bliss with Ezekiel Smith. Although a kind and gentle man, he could be roused on occasion to wrathful anger. No stranger to firearms, he was a dead shot and would not refrain from using any means of furthering what he believed to be right. She could only pray that he did not come here to Breakneck Gap in search of revenge. The horrid cannon fire and the screams of the dying men and horses had upset her more than she had allowed to show. The memory still haunted her. It didn't affect her mind, though, nor her keen intelligence.

Already she had begun to store away details of the layout of the bawdyhouse, the other buildings in town, and where arms and ammunition were stored. She hoped to discover more, and for good reason.

She had seen Eli Holten ahead of the soldiers, during the mad dash for town. Later she had spotted him in the thick of battle. Her heart swelled with hope when she observed his escape to safety. He would be back. She knew it. Even if he did not know of her abduction and that of the other girls, he would return.

With him would come enough soldiers to crush this unspeakable swine, Captain Weatherby, and all his men. When that time came, she wanted to be ready.

Chapter 10

Two drummers kept up a slow, steady rhythm on their large, hide-covered instruments. Other old men chanted songs of greatness in the days gone by, the "grandfather times." Men tall and squat, lean and fat, alike only in their simple clothing of loincloth, leggings and moccasins, arrived in Kicking Elk's camp. Bronze bodies gathered in clusters to talk among themselves, faces grim, demeanor solemn. Each was greeted personally by an equally subdued *Hehaka Cankpe-e*. Warriors came from all the bands.

Here the lodges of the Hunkpapa, there the Oglala, across the mighty circle the tipis of the Teton, Santee, and Brule. The Miniconjou and Yankton made up the fourth side. In the center, the hoop of the Sans Arc. All came to pay respect and be counted for the council that would be held in the great lodge at the center of the rings of tents. The *akicita,* the camp police, kept busy directing new arrivals to their proper hoops, while the *eyanpaha* went about throughout the day crying the names of notables and announcing the big feast for that night, prior to the start of the council. All noted the somber visage of the man who had called them together.

Kicking Elk knew that the army had failed. They had

not removed the whites from the sacred valley where the Sun Dance was to be held. It meant war. Bloody, costly, sure to result in even more depredations against the People, yet it would come. The whites had to be driven out. Many of those assembled had come from small farms or reservations close at hand. Some had already been on the trail for the greatest of power ceremonies. All had dropped other activities and hurried to his summons. And what could he tell them?

That more of their young men would die? Their women and children go cold and hungry into the winter? That once more they had to fight a losing battle against the uncountable numbers of the whites? Thicker than pale maggots crawling on dead meat, the white men came. Each show of resistance only brought more. This he knew. His own Sans Arc lived far away, where they could still taste the heady air of freedom. But what of the others?

A part of him gloried in it, even while the sober side of his personality grew saddened. For the time being, though, he would turn away from such thoughts. What of the *hinziwin,* the golden-haired one who sat in his lodge? his mind chided him. Did her presence influence his judgement?

Rachel Johnson leaned against a woven backrest in the doorway to Kicking Elk's lodge. Her hands worked busily, repairing a pair of moccasins. Her mind kept occupied creating new images for her journal.

A vast encampment rose in the foothills of the black mountains revered by these savages. Called by the powerful war chief, Kicking Elk — or Hehaka Cankpe-e, as it is said in the Dakota lan-

guage — who hosted this reporter in his lodge, representatives of all the mighty Sioux gathered to speak of weighty matters. All was laid out in circles. Circles of conical, circular-based tipis within circles of more lodges. Rumors had come that the Army had been beaten by the criminal element in Breakneck Gap.

This could not be so, your correspondent protested. The powerful war leader paid no heed. We are camped on sacred Sioux land, he made clear to me. If the white soldiers will not abide by the treaty, then it will mean war. This reporter shudders at the prospect, though he feels privileged to be present at so momentous an occasion.

"Look, there is a white woman in Kicking Elk's lodge," one of the representatives declared scornfully.

"She makes herself right at home," his companion complained.

"Is she a captive?" a third inquired.

"Looks more like his wife," grunted the first.

Although she could not understand their language, Rachel knew the comments were about her and, judging by the gestures, they were not complimentary. She chose to ignore them as she compiled sense impressions into glowing words of journalistic prose.

Many among these striking emissaries of the plains do not like the presence of your correspondent among them. Despite this, the story must be told. Under the protection of the war leader, this reporter has an opportunity to observe a spectacle unlike any witnessed by a white man before. Tonight there is to be a feast of welcome. Tomorrow begins the difficult debate on how to deal with the crisis facing the entire Sioux nation.

Such a feast it had turned out to be, Rachel thought to herself as she lay in Kicking Elk's arms long after midnight.

Two buffalo had been located and killed. Their car-

106

casses had been set to roasting, along with that of a medium-sized elk. She had been bathing in the icy creek beyond the village and, mercifully, had not heard or seen the butchering of a dozen dogs. They went into a stew which, in her ignorance, she found to be quite delicious. There had been singing and dancing of such a wild, exhilarating nature that she found it impossible to discover deserving words to describe the festivities.

After the singing ended, she and Kicking Elk had made wild, energetic love for seemingly endless hours. Now she drifted off into sweet dreams, comprised of sexual and gastronomic fantasies.

The sun stood only an hour old when the *eyanpahas* ran through camp announcing the start of the big council. There would be time to eat the first meal and bathe, and then the big drum would summon the participants.

Kicking Elk looked overwhelmingly impressive when he left the lodge for the meeting. Clean from a long spell in the creek, his raven hair sleek and tied into two glossy braids, his face clean of warpaint, bare chest decorated with hanging necklaces of shells, beads, and silver buttons, his best moccasins, leggings, and loin cloth covering his body, he struck a regal figure in Rachel's mind. Without even a grunt in her direction, he took up his lance and walked toward the tall, wide-based council lodge.

After smoking the ritual pipe to the Spirits of the East, South, West, North, Above, and Below, Kicking Elk paused in solemn reflection on what he would say, while the pipe went the rounds of those present. When it returned to his hands, he placed it on its carved rest and rose to speak. His words, though emotional, did not contain the shrill edge of hysteria that usually summoned men to the warpath.

"Men of the Dakota . . . brothers . . . you know of my vision in which the Valley-Where-the-Sky-Fell was pointed out to me by the Great Spirit. It is there that he wishes the Sun Dance to be readied this year. *Hecitu yelo*. You know, too, that *kiyuksa* white men, those who break their own laws, have built a village on that spot. These whites have strong medicine. This I have seen with my eyes and felt with my flesh.

"Many braves of the *Itazipicola* died by the medicine of their long guns that shoot straight. The bullets they shoot spit slivers of metal that cut and tear." Kicking Elk pointed to scabbed-over wounds on his thighs and one shoulder. "We can't make war on them directly. Yet they must be driven from the appointed place. I've called you here to tell you how we must do this.

"First we must close off the only way into the valley. When the white men there see they cannot get food or supplies, they will leave or starve."

A slender young Oglala, leader of the *Cante Tinza* — Brave Heart — warrior society among his tribe, rose politely and waited to be recognized. At a nod from Kicking Elk he spoke.

"We don't have the time to make this effective. In less than one moon, the Sun Dance must be started."

"I know this," Kicking Elk returned, speaking softly and gently. "And my heart is heavy to say these words. If we do not force out the evil white men in the valley, we must make war on all whites. I know that many of you, your families, your villages, will suffer the most if we pursue this course. My people, the *Itazipicola*, are far to the west. The soldiers can't find them, and they will not be punished. It is for you to decide this thing. Having

108

faced the medicine guns of the bad whites, my men are few. It is your blood that will be shed, your ponies that will be ridden into the ground. War with the whites is a path to darkness.

For each one we kill, two hands more come to hunt us. I do not lightly ask you, my brothers, to consider this way. Our time *is* short. Perhaps the total of all our days is shorter than we can imagine. But our way is clear. I sent a message to the pony-soldier chief in the place called Raw-lins. The soldiers came and tried to remove the men in the valley." Kicking Elk paused deliberately to let the full impact hit his audience.

"The soldiers lost."

Cries of surprise and consternation ran around the circle. Never did the soldiers lose.

"Yes. It is true. Now they have ridden away. If they will come back, I do not know. Some say their hearts were not in it because they fought for the Dakota. I cannot tell you if that is true or not. I do know that, of those who rode into the valley, only half came out. If we lost so many in a single battle, would we stay to fight longer?"

"No!" an old man of the Santee shouted out.

"So many, so many soldiers dead," rippled from one tongue to another.

"If the soldiers fail us, we have only ourselves to defend what is ours." A great sadness filled Kicking Elk's voice as he uttered his ultimatum. "To do so, we must take the warpath against all whites. I have spoken."

Heads bowed, shoulders slumped, their uniforms powdered gray-brown from dust, the defeated troopers of Eli Holten's small command walked their jaded horses down the main street of Eagle Pass. Eager calls greeted them, and the fatigued scout found he had to concentrate forcibly on the meaning of the words shouted at them.

"Gone? The girls from the Thunder Saloon?" he asked dazedly.

"Some hardcases came in here," the mayor, and owner of the general mercantile, elaborated. "They killed Hobie Banes and a bunch of customers, dragged the girls out the back door. Had a wagon waiting there. They took the Reverend Smith's wife, too. And a little child named Elizabeth Brewster. This is her father, Judge Brewster."

Eli had halted the troops and stared down now at a portly, distinguished-looking gentleman in a conservatively cut brown suit. His thick mane of silver hair rose majestically, precluding the use of a hat. He had a soft look about him, the scout noted.

Not in the eyes, though. Solid granite shined with determination in his gray orbs, a match to Eli's own flinty gaze. Thin, uncompromising lips parted in a red gash.

"Is the Army going to do something about this?" he demanded.

"Any idea where they were taken?" Holten inquired.

"Sure we know. To the Black Hills. To some valley with a high ring of rugged hills around it."

"Breakneck Gap," the scout breathed out. "Judge Brewster, we've just come back from that valley. This is what's left of two companies. The man who runs Breakneck Gap has two Whitworth cannon up there. From what the late Captain Pierce told me, they have a range of nearly two miles. I know you are anxious about your daughter. I'm concerned for all of them. But, tell me."

110

Eli drew out his words carefully, locked eye to eye in a frosty battle of wills. "Would you take men against those guns, unprotected by artillery?"

"Uh—no, sir. I was an artillery officer in the late war. B Battery, Two-thirty-ninth New York. I am not familiar with the weapon. Yet, from the evidence of your staggering losses, I can only concur. What will you be doing?"

"We have to return to Fort Rawlins, outfit a larger expedition, and come back with artillery."

"In haste, I presume."

"In the utmost hurry, Judge."

"And what about my wife?" a thunderous, evangelical voice inquired.

The Reverend Ezekiel Smith approached the crowd around the soldiers. Townsfolk parted to make way for him as he came to where Eli sat on his horse.

"Hello, Eli. I went looking for you, only to discover you were on your way to where those abominations took my Amy."

"We have been there and back, Reverend Zeke. I was sorry to hear—about Amy."

"What are we going to do about it?"

"We? I'm going back to Fort Rawlins for reinforcements."

"In the meantime, Amy is in that den of thieves and cutthroats. Do you have any doubt as to why they stole women?"

"Uh—no."

"Then it is up to us to get them back, Eli. God has shown that to me."

"We can't simply ride in there and ask for her return, you know."

111

"There has to be a way."

"Sure. A lot of soldiers and some artillery."

"And what happens to those women, to my wife, in the meantime? Or when your soldiers start shelling that town?"

"Unnnh!" The realization hit Eli like a fist in the gut. "Then we have to get them out of there before the cavalry hits the place again."

"Now you're thinking."

"Captain Pierce said we could only take the town by deceit."

"Brilliant. Once we're inside the town, we can get the women out. Has anyone there seen your face?"

"Only at a distance. And in these clothes. I could never get away with riding in and saying howdy."

"You could if you didn't look like yourself," Ezekiel prompted.

"Say, that's right. Most people don't really look at a person's features. They form a general impression of clothing, stance, voice and coloration. In other words, if I were to wear your clerical collar, or Judge Brewster's judicial robes, no one would recognize me as Chief Scout of the Twelfth. In fact, I think that gives me an idea on how we might, if we're lucky, get into Breakneck Gap."

Chapter 11

"What is this again?" Rachel Johnson asked in badly-accented Lakota, her voice teasing as she squeezed Kicking Elk's flaccid penis.

"That is my *sluka*," he told her laughingly.

"And what is it now?" she pressed, rapidly stroking it to erectness.

"*Cežin.*"

"How is that used?"

"Like this . . . and this . . ." Kicking Elk murmured as he buried his bigness between her lush breasts, then slid its sensitive tip down her silken belly to the thick thatch of yellow hair that covered her pouting mound.

"And like this," he added as he buried the engorged tip in the lacy outer folds of her moist, fevered purse.

"*Hiye-hey-i-i!*" she squealed as he penetrated her moist portal and thrust deeply into her furnace-like passage.

In the short while she had been in the warcamp of Kicking Elk's Sans Arc Sioux, Rachel had become deeply involved in the role of a white squaw. In her mind she saw herself with a cradle board on her back, with an obsidian-eyed little baby boy resting there, an exact miniature image of his dear father. She already knew how to mend buckskin clothing, moccasins, and tipi covers. She could skin a rabbit, butcher a buffalo haunch, and find wild onions for a stew. With no other women in camp, she had nothing by which to gauge her experience.

In her ignorance, she had no idea of the arduous existence led by Sioux wives and mothers. Nor had she any conception of how children were expected to be raised. The youngest person in camp was a boy, sort of an apprentice warrior, she guessed, of perhaps thirteen or fourteen. Small for his size, she wanted to mother him. *He* wanted to make her a mother.

Day or night, when not occupied by other duties, he followed her about making wistful sighs. His eyes filled with distant longing, his lips curved in a silly grin, and his breechcloth bulged with his excitement, he idolized her and shyly courted her favor. For her own part, Rachel encouraged him.

At Kicking Elk's invitation, all the other braves had sampled her one time each. Not that she had minded that. A lot were better than none at all. Only the boy had been excluded. *Mastincola* was his name. It meant Little Rabbit, she knew. If the size of that bulge meant anything, he wasn't all *that* little. He was so *cute*. If only she could find a way to take him away with her when Eli Holten came to rescue her. They could have a great deal of fun together, while he learned the ways of love instead of war.

"You're a sick woman," Rachel's mind chided her. "He's only a child."

But with a pleasure prod big enough to satisfy a Percheron mare, her seamier side disputed.

Until that time, she mused as she melted in the delightful fluidity of Kicking Elk's lovemaking, she would

114

have to content herself with what she had. Or at least until she could get *Mastincola* alone somewhere.

Captain William Weatherby paced the floor of his office and glanced out the window. Seated nearby, Freddy Mullins watched his leader closely and tried to figure out what this meeting had been called to discuss.

"We may have run the Army off, Freddy, but the Sioux are entirely another matter. They are too primitive and ignorant to know when they are beaten. I want you to take six men and make a sweep through the area. Locate those Indians, and find out what they are planning to do."

"Aye-aye, Cap'n. If I may speak, sir, there's something besides the Sioux that's worrying me."

"Yes, Freddy. What is that?"

"The Army. I think you're takin' them too lightly. They aren't limited to sabres, carbines and pistols, you know. What if they bring artillery down on us?"

"We destroy their guns before they can fire."

"Not all of them, sir. I know a little about cavalry, Cap'n. They have these little six-pounder guns called gallopers. And some Napoleons on light carriages. They don't fire in battery. They use 'em wherever they need 'em to support the troops. Our Whitworths can only shoot one direction at a time."

"Ummmm. Quite right, Freddy. I was, ah, aware of the problem, of course. Simply didn't give it enough thought. What would you suggest?"

"I'd put one gun out of town. Someplace where it would provide interlocking fire on the entrance to the gap and also be able to shoot over the buildings at any field pieces they managed to get through and free enough to move."

"Capital! I'll see to it while you're gone. And thank you, Freddy."

"It's nothing, sir."

Freddy Mullins set about his task in a thoughtful mood. Old Weatherby might be hell on the waves in a ship, but land fighting simply wasn't his game. If he kept up like this, it could be an easy matter smoothly to take over the whole operation. There was a lot of money to be made entertaining badmen. Weatherby did all right by himself already. With the connections he himself had, Freddy considered, he might be able to double that within a year. First, though, he would have to come up with a means of pacifying the Army and working out some sort of agreement that would let them stay in the valley.

Rachel Johnson luxuriated in the chill water of the little stream outside Kicking Elk's camp. As she washed her fevered body, she trembled with a chill of excitement. She had managed to convey to Little Rabbit that he was to join her here. A small stab of guilt ran through her.

After all, he was only a boy. What she proposed was shameful. Yet, in these primal surroundings, among these primitive people, it somehow seemed to be all right. Perhaps he would not come.

She gave a little start of surprise when *Mastincola* stepped through the screen of willows and appeared on the muddy bank. Swiftly he removed his moccasins and breech cloth. Rachel quickly forgot any reservations her conscience had built for her.

Fully man-sized, despite his age and small stature, his

116

rigid organ protruded out, curving slightly upward, from his slender form. He smiled shyly and walked a ways into the water.

"I have come," he announced.

"I am glad. Get closer to me. I want to touch you."

Rachel's eyes devoured the handsome, clean-limbed boy as he surged out to thigh depth in the creek. She ached to get her hands on that reddish, swollen member that bobbed and swayed before her. Tentatively, shy as a young girl, she reached for it.

Other eyes than Rachel's watched the scene at the bathing place. Great hunger grew in Freddy Mullins' chest as he eyed the voluptuous beauty of the blonde reporter's ample body. His breath quickened, and he could sense an increase in the speed of his heart.

"That one's built for comfort, rather'n speed," he whispered to the man next to him. "Like a big ol' brood mare."

Rachel's hand closed around the slender Indian boy's erect penis. He giggled and reflexively jerked away from the contact. Eagerly, Rachel pursued, taking him in hand again. She began to stroke him. Her words, though in Lakota, reached Freddy and the men on the overhanging bank.

"What a pretty *sluka* on so small a boy. Do you like *ceazin*?"

Little Rabbit giggled again and answered breathily, "Yes."

Rachel quickly knelt before him and encircled his narrow bony waist with one arm. With her other hand, she guided his throbbing staff to her lips.

"By God, that gal's gonna gobble the kid's knob!" a Breakneck Gap hardcase blurted out.

117

"Shusssh!" Freddy cautioned. "Let 'em get really worked up. Then we're gonna take that pretty thing back as a present for Cap'n Weatherby. Might be she can tell us what the redsticks have in mind. Go on honey," he whispered encouragement to Rachel. "Take him all in. Make the li'l beggar glassy-eyed."

It took longer than Freddy had expected it might.

Rachel, too, discovered that Little Rabbit was no stranger to this sort of attention. He knew how to pace himself and cautioned her to relax several times in order to prolong the delightful experience. It heightened her enjoyment likewise.

Then the Sioux boy began to gasp. He threw his head back and wriggled in her slippery embrace. Rachel gave it her all. With a powerful thrust of his hips, Little Rabbit reached his completion. Rachel moaned mightily as he gushed out his life force.

She quaked as her own body came into the grips of a mighty climax.

"Now!" Freddy commanded.

Strong arms grabbed Rachel from behind. The pulsing organ in her mouth jerked away violently and she had room to scream.

"Shut her up, dammit!" Freddy yelled as he pulled Little Rabbit to one side.

The Indian boy writhed and fought his captor, one hand reaching for the knife that was not at his side. Freddy found his, though, and drove it deep into *Mastincola's* taut abdomen. The tip penetrated smoothly, once past the rigid muscles, and bit upward to pierce the boy's diaphragm.

Blood squirted in crimson profusion as Freddy pulled his blade free. Rachel screamed again.

"Hehaka Cankape-e!" she called in Lakota. "Help!"

Shouts of alarm rose in the camp. Rustling in the brush told the invaders they had little time. Freddy balled one fist and clipped Rachel along the right side of her jaw. She gasped a tiny sigh and went limp in the arms of the hardcase who held her. Quickly they ran along the streambed to the point where they had left their horses.

Kicking Elk and three braves appeared on the bank at the bathing place as the cutthroats from Breakneck Gap climbed through the willows and hurriedly mounted up. Red rage fogged the war leader's vision as he looked down at the corpse of little *Mastincola*. The realization came that the yellow-haired woman had been carried away by whoever had attacked the pair at their trysting place.

"Get horses. We will follow them," he commanded.

The chase carried them to the entrance of the narrow passage to Breakneck Gap. There the Sans Arc warriors turned off and reined in. Seething with impotent rage, Kicking Elk glowered at the retreating white men.

"Sons without fathers," he cursed. "They have murdered a small boy and carried off my woman. They will be made to pay."

"It's good riddance, I say," one of the braves observed. "She fed your trust in the soldiers too much."

Kicking Elk turned a mask of naked fury on him. "You say too much! Is there any doubt these men are evil? We must defeat them, medicine guns or not. Come, we will talk again in council."

"I got me a real prize here," Freddy chortled. "The Cap'n thanked me right polite like and returned her to

119

me, after he'd questioned her. Man-of-man, am I ever gonna wear myself out on this one." He patted Rachel on her ample buttocks.

"Keep your hands off me, you bastard!" the lady reporter snarled.

Freddy continued to parade the captured white girl around Breakneck Gap. He called her his little white squaw and used every means to humiliate her.

"Yep," he told one group of British gunners. "She's almost too hot to handle. She musta gone through all them redskins till they couldn't get it up any more. She was suckin' off some little Injun kid when I caught her."

"You pig! You filthy slime!" Rachel wailed in desperate futility.

Gradually her mind withdrew from the humiliation of the present. She began to compose blazing lines of journalistic brilliance.

Late one afternoon, the Sioux village where this reporter visited was attacked by a band of white brigands. They swept in past the camp police and attacked in force. Your correspondent quickly took up arms and joined his newfound friends in defense of their lodges. After furious fighting, this reporter was captured by the frontier riff-raff. Imagine your correspondent's amazement to discover that the destination of these hardened criminals was the very town that the cavalry had been sent to clean out.

"The Army!" Freddy roared at a drunken ruffian in the next saloon. "The Army ain't comin' back here. You can count on that. Not with the lickin' we gave them."

The Army—defeated? Rachel's thoughts grew desperate, and she longed for paper and pen to record all the strange impressions this outlaw town of Breakneck Gap flooded over her. A sudden noisy disturbance outside drew her interest.

A wagon, with two saddle horses tied to the tailgate and an odd-looking cargo aboard, slowly rolled along the main street that led from the trail through the gap. A tall, fiercely evangelical man in shirtsleeves, with black clerical collar and bib, sat at a foot-pumper organ. Body moving in time with the music, he cranked out the familiar notes of a popular hymn.

"Lead, kin-dly light . . ." Two voices rose in the lyrics as the unusual vehicle neared the center of the small community.

"Hallelujah!" the man at the organ called out when the music ended. "Salvation has come to Breakneck Gap. Praise the Lord, boys. I'm here to extend the love of God into your sinful and sordid lives. I'm the Reverend Ezekiel Piker, and this is my able assistant, Deacon Jones."

Rachel could not believe her eyes. Seated behind the reins, wearing a Roman collar and black bib, black frock coat and rounded, preacher's hat, was Eli Holten.

Chapter 12

"Yea, brothers, I have come among you to bring the salvation of God's word to this nest of sinners. It is my mission to do this, because of my openly admitted station in life. For I am a sinner, too," the Reverend Ezekiel Smith thundered in his best evangelical tone. He stood in the middle of the wagon bed, long, black frock coat unbuttoned and flapping in a slight breeze. With graceful, familiar clerical gestures of arms and hands, he emphasized his words as they tumbled onto his astonished audience.

"Over the years of my ministry, I have been thrown out of every decent, God-fearing community I set foot in. And why, brothers? Because I refuse to be a hypocrite!

"When the labors of the day are done, I like to savor a bit of the fruits of John Barleycorn. There are some who take offense at that." That brought some laughs and a mutter of agreement. "I am fond of the ladies, but am owned by no single one. Many good Christians find that offensive to their sense of righteousness."

"There's nothin' wrong with that, preacher," one hardcase quipped.

"If the church collections fall short, I find it not at all improper to make up the difference by a small withdrawal from the strongbox on a Wells Fargo coach. Hardly a soul exists who does not find that reprehensible. Yet the Good Book says that we are all sinners. Who, then, am I to make a liar out of God?" Ezekiel paused to let this revelation sink into the slower minds around him.

"If a man admits he is a sinner, but walks with God, he had found the way to salvation. Let Him see you in church on Sunday, and He'll forgive you when He sees you riding another man's horse. Give generously to the support of the House of the Lord, and He'll not fault you for obtaining your money from a bank where you have no account. Why, with the right sort of attitude, you can please God while you plunder the golden gates of Heaven!"

"Well, I never . . ." a wondering voice declared from the crowd.

"Did you ever see the likes?" another inquired.

"He's sure a pistol, ain't he?"

Ezekiel raised his hands for silence once again. "Rejoice, brothers. I am the Reverend Ezekiel Piker, and this is my able assistant, Deacon Jones. We have come to bring peace and solace to your troubled souls. We have also come to establish a church among our own kind. Verily I say unto you . . ."

Captain William Weatherby stood at the window of his office, watching intently through the lace curtain. He had heard the arrival of the two unusual evangelists and paused in his work to take in what they might have to say. He soon found himself nodding in agreement with the words of this Reverend Piker, though all reason told him to reject his premise out of hand. The man had to be insane. His thesis was totally wrong. But his twisted logic appealed to the blunted sensitivities of the lawless men in Breakneck Gap.

Such a man could be useful, the former Royal Navy officer concluded. And Piker wanted to build a church here. The presence of that institution would add a touch of respectability to the town. It would please Marilee, also. Weatherby made his decision.

When the preacher finished his harangue, he would summon the newcomers and sound them out a bit.

Amy Smith lay naked on her bed. She felt unclean, and her situation still tormented her soul. It left her time to think over what she had learned about Breakneck Gap and the mad Britisher who ran the town.

It didn't amount to a lot. Naturally, all of the inmates of the brothels had been abducted at one time or another. None desired to remain. If she designed some means of escape, they could be counted on to flee, too. It would create quite a bit of confusion. Most of all, she wanted to help her friends and former co-workers from the Thunder Saloon. A hesitant knock at the door interrupted her planning. She quickly covered herself with a thin dressing gown.

"Who is it?"

"Mister Tandy, Miss. Geoffrey Tandy."

Amy thought of the young boy whom Captain Weatherby called *Mister* Tandy. Relieved that it wasn't another customer, she rose and crossed the room.

"Come in, Geoffrey."

"Thank you, Miss."

"Take a seat," Amy directed as she pointed out a worn loveseat near the window. "What is it brings you here?"

"I—well, I have, er, this problem that, ah, I would like—like to talk over with you," the small boy stammered.

"What is that?"

"I w-would like—ah, to, er, know h-how to go about, ah, courting Miss Elizabeth."

Suddenly Amy found herself liking this shy boy a great deal. She also knew he had other things on his mind.

"What you mean is, can I help you find a way to get into her drawers?"

Tandy's cheeks flushed and he lowered his eyes. "Oh, no. Er—that is—yes. Only, h-how can you tell?"

"From that bulge in the front of your trousers, Geoffrey." Amy swiftly reached out and playfully tweaked the rigid protrusion in Geoffrey's tight, white trousers. It promptly withered.

A flood of crimson colored Geoffrey's face. He squirmed on the small couch and nibbled at a fragment of fingernail. "She's really such a beautiful girl, is she not? And—I had hoped, I thought that maybe . . ." he ended in a helpless shrug.

"Don't get your hopes up too high. Elizabeth Brewster is such a prim and proper young lady. She would be horrified at your designs on her, ah, body."

"Oh, but she gave me a secret note. Asked me to come to her room later this afternoon. Alone. She made a point of my being alone."

This piece of intelligence surprised Amy. Since the Brewsters had taken up residence in Eagle Pass to wait discharge of their eldest son from the army, young Elizabeth had been a loud and vocal opponent of nearly every aspect of life in the prairie community. Particularly anything that might have even the slightest hint of impropriety.

"Tell me, what is it, exactly, that you propose to do at

125

this secret meeting? A child of your age, do you even know what it's about?"

"Oh, yes," Geoffrey returned quickly.

"Suppose you tell me."

"But—I mean, you're a woman!" he protested, shocked and blushing furiously at the prospect.

"Look at me, Geoffrey. Where are we? Surely you are aware of what we do in this place? Believe me, there's little you might say that could shock me."

Tandy took a deep breath. "Well then, a—a m-man puts his, er, you-know-what inside a woman's special place—and, er—that's what it's all about, don't you see?"

Amy smiled patiently. "That's not exactly the most graphic description I've ever heard. It'll do for the basics, though. Only you forgot one important part."

"What's that?"

"You have to move it around."

"Eh? How's that?"

"Slide it back and forth. Like this." Amy made a hollow fist of her right hand and enclosed her left index finger in it. Then she began to stroke the latter into the former.

"There, you see? That's where the good feeling comes from. Surely you know something about that?"

"Oh, yes," Geoffrey responded, suddenly growing more confident. "I learned abou that a long while ago." Then his embarrassment flooded over him once more. "Only it's supposed to be different—and better—when you, ah, well, you know, when it's done with a girl instead of by yourself."

"You're a sweet boy, Geoffrey. Only, since you have all the essential facts down, what did you come to me for?"

"Well, I thought—perhaps—since I've never—done that with a girl before, that you might—"

Revelation dawned on Amy. Her eyes went wide and twinkled with merriment. "Why, that's very flattering, Geoffrey. But, why did you select me to, ah, initiate you into the mysteries, so to speak?"

"You are very lovely, Miss. And—I've heard talk—" He cleared his throat. "After all, as you said, this is that sort of place. And so I thought it a good idea to come to you for, ah, instruction."

Amy reached out and patted his cheek. "How darling of you. But you should know, I am a married woman. I'm not here of my own free will, and I only do, ah, what I have to when I'm forced into it. Don't despair, though. I think I know just the thing to help you."

Geoffrey brightened. "You do? What . . . how . . .?"

"Calm down. There's a little Sioux girl right down the hall. Not much older than you, as a matter of fact. She takes to this work with a sort of natural zeal. I'm sure she would be happy to guide and instruct you in the secret arts of love."

"Really! That would be smashing! Oh, Miss, this makes me feel so much better. I can't ever find words enough to thank you."

Amy gave him a cool, sisterly kiss on one cheek and rose to leave. "I'll be back in a moment."

Amy's nearness, her heady scent, and Geoffrey's excitable imagination had their effect while the Reverend Smith's wife was out of the room. Geoffrey soon found himself every bit as achingly erect as he had been when he entered Amy's apartment. Unfortunately, anticipation coupled with boyish inexperience soon undid him.

As Geoffrey fumbled with his tightly stretched trousers to ease his discomfort, the vivid images that danced in his mind exercised their magic effect. A flood of warmth filled his underdrawers and pooled about the base of his pulsing organ. Humiliated by this secret display, he let a sob of misery escape his lips. By the time Amy returned, he had sunk into deep depression.

"There now. It's all arranged."

"Fat lot of good it'll do," Geoffrey wailed. He wanted to cry.

"Oh? How's that?"

"I went and—and made a sticky mess of things, just *thinking* about it."

"Is that all? Believe me, that won't hurt a thing. At your age, it shouldn't take any time at all to be ready again. Why, all little Willow Frond will have to do is reach out and touch you, and you'll be amazed at what you can do."

"Do you really think so?"

"Of course," Amy reassured him.

Shyly, Geoffrey leaned toward her and kissed her on the lips. "You've been absolutely marvelous to me, Miss. Thank you ever so much."

"You're welcome. Now, hurry along. She's waiting for you. Quite anxiously, I might add. She can't understand why you've waited so long."

"My—oh, my. It's—it's working already," Geoffrey cried excitedly as he hurried from the room.

Alone again, Arm's thoughts went back to her predicament. She knew that the Army, and Eli Holten, had been here and that Weatherby's men had driven them off. The Sioux had attacked, too. The girls of the Thunder Saloon were more than ready to escape. They had all been too busy over the past few days to lay any active plans. Besides, being new, they were watched closely. No matter the indignities she had to endure, she had to bide her time. Half an hour had passed in such considerations when she heard Geoffrey's triumphal yell from down the hall.

"I did it! I really bloody well did it. And it felt *wonderful*!"

A short time later, Sylvia entered her room, her face aglow with the excitement generated by the news she bore.

"You'll never believe it, Amy. I was so shocked, I didn't for a while."

"What is it, Sylvia?"

"Reverend Zeke is here."

"My husband?" A cold dread filled Amy's heart. "Is—is he alone?"

"No. There's another man with him. A, ah, Deacon Jones. Reverend Zeke is calling himself Reverend Piker."

"I hope he doesn't intend to do anything foolish. The man with him. Could it be Eli?"

"I don't know for sure, Amy. He is tall, with big shoulders. I only saw him for a moment from behind. They're on the way to that awful Captain Weatherby's office."

"We'll have to wait and see, then," Amy told her distractedly. Already her mind worked on new plans for escape, this time including her husband.

Eli Holten stood a step inside the doorway to Captain William C. Weatherby's office. He wore a black suit with a dicky and Roman collar, and he clutched a dowdy black hat in his hands. His long, yellow locks had been shorn short enough to expose his slightly large ears. The loose coat covered his holstered revolver and the Bowie on his left side. Over by the large, highly polished desk, Zeke Smith had taken a chair at the former officer's invitation.

"Now, then," the captain commenced after the preliminaries had ended. "Let's make the situation entirely clear. For a town to be entirely successful, it is necessary for it to have saloons, bordellos and at least one church. The latter must be in touch with the needs and moral climate of the community. That last is most important.

"These are rough men here. None of them could qualify for sainthood."

"Neither can we, Captain," Zeke boomed back. "Ain't many sins that Deacon Jones there an' me have overlooked in our lives. We understand the sort of ruffian and villainous customer one gets in an isolated frontier outpost such as this. They can understand us, too. That way we can spread the word of Gawd to them with ease."

Weatherby smiled coldly. "Let's dispense with that, Reverend, and get down to facts. You propose to build a church, for which, I shall provide the land. Building materials are at a premium. I'm afraid you'll not have much to choose from except dirt and lodge pole pines. The latter you can acquire on the fringes of the valley."

"Even a log cabin is suitable to house the altar of God. When can we begin construction, Brother Weatherby?"

"As soon as you have your first converts. Now, there are a few regulations." Weatherby went on to explain about murder, rape, and robbery. Then he covered defense of the town. In conclusion, he added, "We run things the British way here, all neat and tidy. You will be required to keep your arms at the magazine. In the event of an emergency, they shall be issued to you."

"No, sir," Ezekiel snapped. "As a servant of God, I must be prepared to defend His sanctuary against any invasion at all times. I keep my guns, and so does Deacon Jones."

"I'm afraid that's not possible."

"It's the only way. You want a church, an' we want to build one. But we've done rather well with our weapons at our sides, and we aim to continue doing so."

"Well . . ." Captain Weatherby began to weaken his resolve. "Considering that you are the clergy, I suppose an exception could be made. But for you gentlemen only. Wouldn't do to have the common rabble running around armed, now, would it?"

"Oh, quite, quite," Eli added facetiously from the doorway. "Wouldn't it be nice if the same could be arranged for towns away from here, where someone might want to rob a bank or two?"

"Right, then," Weatherby rushed on, ignoring the scout's barb. "There's another consideration. What's in this church thing for me?"

Gotcha! Reverend Smith thought with glee. "Why, the satisfaction of aiding the salvation of your fellow men. That — and ten percent of the take on collections and special donations."

"That's not at all what I was after. Make it fifteen percent," Weatherby offered back.

"Done."

"We're in business, then. You may begin at any time."

"There's one other little consideration to be made. In my oration, I mentioned that I had a fondness for the ladies. Considering your, ah, major occupation here, I would like your permission to sample some of the wares and — er, make my choice."

"Nothing easier. Feel free to do so. Take one, a pair, sample all of them if you desire. Ah! Women — God's greatest gift to man. I dearly love them, myself. All of them. So make yourself at home, Reverend Piker."

"Thank you, Captain Weatherby. Do you — I mean,

would you mind giving me something in writing so that your minions understand our agreement between, ah, gentlemen?"

"Not at all. I'll draft you something later today."

At the moment, an attractive young woman entered the office. Her trim, shapely body could not be disguised by the voluminous skirts and lace bodice of her blouse. She turned sea-green eyes on first the Reverend Smith, then Eli Holten. They widened slightly at the sight of the scout, then turned to the man behind the desk.

"Hello, Father. I thought I would come see our new visitors."

"Reverend, Deacon, this is my daughter, Marilee. Marilee, the Reverend Piker and his assistant, Deacon Jones."

"Charmed," the lovely lass murmured. Again her eyes rested smolderingly on Eli Holten.

"They are going to start a church here in Breakneck Gap," Weatherby continued.

"How simply wonderful. Then I'll have a chance to go to church for the first time, after years in this awful wilderness."

"We will be delighted to have you as a parishioner, Miss Weatherby," Reverend Zeke purred.

"I will be so pleased myself. And I will have to get to know you better, Deacon Jones," Marilee said in a tone that could have been taken for a promise.

None of the other three in the room noticed the dark, thunderous scowl that Capt. William Weatherby directed at his daughter and the man she addressed.

After servicing two ugly, incredibly smelly buffalo hunters, Rachel Johnson wrestled with her conscience.

The distasteful encounters had been quick enough, granted. She had always believed that any man was better than none, but not these ignorant, violent scum who rutted like wild dogs—and in the same position. Somehow she had to escape from this place. The story she had compounded in her head had suddenly swelled to incredible proportions. She *had* to get away from here so the world would know! Rachel roused herself and located paper and pencil.

Quickly the words began to spill out. *Imagine the consternation of this reporter when he discovered that more lay behind this town of criminals than any mere outlaw stronghold. A secret British invasion of our beloved country is under way, directed by an officer of the Royal Navy, Captain William C. Weatherby. Breakneck Gap serves as a recruiting station for ruffians, adventurers, and mercenary soldiers, to fill the ranks of a force destined to try the greatest powers of America's valiant army. To feed the unwholesome appetite of this horde of invaders, women of several nationalities and races are being held against their will, forced to live the most horrible of lives and to be repeatedly subjected to that 'fate worse than death.'*

Only today, your correspondent discovered that all is not lost. Acting undercover, in the guise of an itinerant cleric, the intrepid scout, Eli Holten, was seen in the town. It can only mean that a confrontation is in the making. Your reporter will remain on the scene so that you may have a first-hand account of this momentous conflict between the secret forces of the English Crown and the free men of America.

Chapter 13

Once out on the street, Eli Holten looked askance at his companion. "If I didn't know you better, I'd swear that was the way you ran your regular church work."

"It takes all kinds, Eli," the Reverend Smith replied. "Back in the days before I had my Call, I sold the same bridge over the Potomac to three different congressmen. Funny part was, they all 'owned' it at the same time. Nearly brought about a three-way duel. It was also the reason for my decision to move westward. I worked as a medicine drummer for a while. I made nearly as much out of that muddy, sour-tasting mixture of alcohol and ditchwater as I did from the shell game I ran on the side. People, my friend Eli, will buy anything if you make the package attractive enough."

"That may be. For now, I want to get a better look at the care they give those Whitworths."

"And now that I have this little note from the good captain, I want to go look for my wife."

"I'll meet you at the hotel in three hours. That'll give me a chance to look after the horses, too," the scout told him.

Eli Holten strolled the short block of the main street to the big round brick tower of the magazine building.

He received several amused and, to his surprise, more than a few respectful greetings from the rough-edged denizens of Breakneck Gap. He tried to make his examination appear casual. One of the deadly field pieces had been drawn outside to be cleaned, and its brightwork polished. As the crew labored on it, he drew closer.

A most unusual piece. It had a fat breech, nearly pear-shaped, he observed. A rifled barrel, and the unusual inertial starter device for the screw-threaded breechblock. Overall, it looked to him as though anyone familiar with artillery pieces could load and fire it. Hitting something might be another matter.

"You there, deacon," a ragged Cockney voice called to him. "Are ye fixin' to baptize these guns?"

"It would do no harm, would it? A little water might keep the breech cooler."

A chorus of friendly laughter rose from the stained and greasy gun handlers. Holten stepped closer and managed to peer into the cavernous main floor of the armory.

The other Whitworth was not there. The surprise jolted him. Where had it been taken? He would have to find out, but not now, on his first day in town. He raised one hand over the men in what he hoped to be a gesture of benediction and started down the side street to the livery stable.

When Eli reached the barn, he found the owner and stable boy off to a late midday meal. The scout went to the stalls assigned to Sonny, his big Morgan stallion, and to the reverend's mount, Erasmus. Both had ample rations of oats, and fresh hay had been forked into the mangers. He started for the communal corral behind the building, where the wagon mounts had been quartered, when a small, soft hand on his shoulder arrested movement.

"Well, we meet again, deacon."

Eli turned to look into the provocative sea-green eyes of Marilee Weatherby. She wore a tight blouse now, far more revealing than anything remotely acceptable to the standards of any other community. It made a major production out of her full, lush breasts and emphasized the narrow perfection of her waist. Flaring hips held up a whipcord riding skirt in a soft, doe-eye brown, piped with darker sable trim. She batted long lashes and waited for his reaction.

The scout disappointed her, if she expected some extreme demonstration of emotion. He smiled slightly, briefly, and allowed his eyes to take in every impression of figure and appearance. His expression revealed that he liked what he saw.

"Hello, Miss Weatherby. Have you been here long?"

"No. I came looking for you. And, please, call me Marilee."

"Gladly, Marilee. I'm, ah, Eli," the scout gave her for lack of anything more original. "What was it you wanted? Your father, perhaps?"

"No. He didn't send me with any message. In fact, he'd bloody well have a fit if he knew I was here. Go right bonkers. It's for me. *I* wanted to come here and see you. You see, we share a great secret."

"Oh? What is that?"

"Your name confirmed my suspicions. Be advised, Eli Holten, Chief Scout of the Twelfth Cavalry, I saw your brave exploit in rescuing that poor wounded officer in the battle outside town. I thought that was a magnificent gesture."

For a moment, even though words of praise, Marilee's speech sent a chill of danger through the scout's big frame. One small slip by this desirable young lady could bring him and Ezekiel Smith instant death. He paused a moment to consider while he shaped his reply.

"Oh, did you? While your father's men chewed us into globs of fuzzy red flesh, you watched and cheered the Army on?"

"Something like that. At least, I thought you the most handsome and dashing of men. But don't worry. I won't tell Father about you. That will be our secret. Provided—"

"What sort of conditions do you have in mind?"

"Only that you show me a lot of friendly attention while you're here. We don't get many nice men here in Breakneck Gap. Most of them are worse than mad dogs. I—a girl gets lonely. I'm sure you understand what I mean?"

"Uh, yes. As a matter of fact, I think I'm a bit ahead of you," Eli told her as his ample member began to distend and stiffen. No matter the danger, or her father's many faults and arrogant assurance of his own rightness, she remained a lovely and desirable young woman. Eli felt his pulse quicken and tasted a familiar tanginess on his tongue.

Marilee's hungry expression summed up her own position eloquently, without an additional word.

"Is there somewhere we can go?" the scout asked.

"Here's good enough. Tate and Barkley won't be back for another hour or two at least. The old man takes a snooze in the afternoons, and that hot-pants little Jimmy Barkley goes sniffing around the younger girls at the bawdyhouses. Not that he can afford to get anything from them. He has to go finish off by hand. But I can promise you a far better bargain than that."

"I'm sure of that. The hayloft, then?"

"A marvelous idea!" Marilee enthused. She clapped her hands in a small-girl gesture and started toward the ladder,

137

made of strips of one-by-four nailed to a six-by-six support post.

Eli lifted Marilee off her feet and started up the rungs effortlessly, the willing young woman in his arms. She squealed in delight. He cast a quick look over the mound of loose stacked hay and located an inviting indentation partway toward the dusty, cobwebbed rafters. He made his way there while Marilee clung to his neck and licked the curlicues behind his left ear.

He set her free, and it took only breathless seconds for her to remove the riding outfit and reveal a flawless, peaches-and-cream body of enticing proportions and scintillating curvatures. Eli's manhood had grown large and insistent. It strained to obtain freedom, to romp among the opulent fields of Marilee's treasure trove. Swiftly he liberated his engorged staff, and it swayed in time to an unheard melody.

"Oooh, how utterly beautiful," Marilee cooed at the sight of it. She rose and clasped his knees with her agile arms so she could kiss the raging, dark-skinned monster. Chill bumps appeared on her perfect skin as she did, and Holten too shuddered with delight.

"Come to me," she begged. "Here . . . now." Her hand played idly with the thatch of yellow strands that only partially covered her swollen, widening mound.

The cleft spread apart, and she followed suit with her legs. With such a sweet-scented invitation, the scout could not refuse. He dropped to his knees and looked upon her peerless, satiny skin with true and deep appreciation. Both of her hands wrapped around the solid extension of his maleness and began to massage energetically. She squeezed and stroked, pulled and cranked it like a wringer.

"Oh, my, there's still quite a bit of it left, isn't there?" she

138

observed with pleasure. Then she popped the remainder into her delicate, hungry mouth and began to lick and slurp upon her newfound, wholesome treat. The hairy sack below his thick root began to sway and slap against her chin, and it made her chuckle deep in her throat.

Great waves of ecstasy washed over the scout as she did this. He longed to bury his fullness deep within that juicy target that continued to give off delightful aromas attesting to its readiness. At last Marilee could contain her own needs no longer. She used the long appendage as a leash to guide her panting lover to the center of her universe.

Holten let himself be directed, thrilling to the way the individual hairs and each leafy ridge gave him a personal and tingling welcome. He ground his hips into her and felt his massive tube plunge beyond the tight ring of the final portal. Down . . . down . . . down he plummeted until he strained to gain but a fraction of an inch more in a passageway grown graspingly tight and heated furnace hot. Then Marilee lunged to meet his assault.

With no attempt to parry, she took the full force of his blade. Impaled on a raging plunger, she clasped her legs around his bare buttocks and clung to his back with neatly manicured nails.

"Oooh! Never . . . had . . . anything . . . so . . . big . . . beFORE!" She grunted out as the scout plowed her fallow fields with a rod of iron.

"I like it. Oh, I like that . . ." Eli murmured in her ear as she began to use concealed muscles to milk him like a prize Jersey.

The tempo of their unheard orchestra increased as they labored up the delirious path to mutual explosion. When it came, cymbals clashed, tympanies rumbled, bells rang, rockets burst, and a mighty chorus sang praises in infinite wonder.

"Ah, you're the best, Eli. The absolute best." Her trembling, hungry mouth went once again to the thick member that sprouted from his body. She closed over it and worked industriously to draw out every final bit of sap that remained. When she had raised it from semi-retirement to full activity once more, she placed her small, glowing face next to his.

"Could you, do you think? Could you actually do so well again?"

"For you, Marilee, I can do anything."

Convinced by her stellar performance in their first mating, the scout wasted no time in beginning the tender, compelling extras that made the final culmination so indescribably wonderful. Marilee found clever ways of answering each challenge with a new puzzle, so that they climbed the peaks and breezed down the valleys of sensual excess until a hazy, syrupy oblivion took charge of them, and they joined together in mutual friction and strain.

Wailing in delight, Marilee climaxed three times before the sweating, laboring scout began to ascend the final pinnacle. He shivered from the cascade of unending pleasure and strove to give equally for all he got. At last, he realized he had nearly met his match in this untutored child of the wilderness. For all her enthusiasm and skill, she revealed a certain naivete that indicated a limited experience with men, or a limited number of lovers. All the same, what she lacked in polish, she made up for in energy.

Her hips ground into him, and he slammed his huge phallus deeply as his head of steam grew with each stroke. At last the boiler could no longer hold the pressure, and a shrill whistle shrieked in his head, as he blanked out completely in tiny, limb-weakening shudders while spurts of his life-force drenched the cavern of the wriggling girl beneath him. Marilee howled her way to yet another climax as he slowly withdrew.

"That we'll have to do again," Eli told her after they regained some fragment of composure.

"I'll hold you to that promise. You can be sure. Only when?"

"What about . . . right . . . now?" Eli suggested as his manly organ began to quicken with new life and rise toward her silken belly.

"Jolly good idea, I'd say. Come to me, my mighty stallion, and split me apart."

"Gladly," he agreed, sliding deeply within her reddened and burning crevice.

"What a lovely collection of damsels you have here," the Reverend Ezekiel Smith informed the madam of the first of Breakneck Gap's three bordellos. "They're like a band of angels, fallen out of heaven, to delight us mortals."

"Them's mighty fancy words, Rev'ren'. But the girls will thank you for them. Any one of them suit your immediate fancy?"

Ezekiel pulled a face. "No. Not exactly. I'm only . . . ah, shall we say, looking over the field for the time being. But I'll be back. Never you fear."

Three of the Thunder Saloon girls stood to one side looking at the visitor. It had taken mighty self-control to avoid blurting out his name or giving any sign that they knew him. He turned to them now and raised his hand in benediction.

" 'Prepare thou the way of deliverance,' " the good reverend intoned. " 'For the hour is near at hand.' Good-bye to all of you. I shall return."

Happy, if surprised and familiar, faces greeted him at the second establishment he visited. To his disappointment, though, the delightful bevy of Thunder Saloon soiled doves did not include his wife. He jollied the madam and two bouncers for a while, commented that he was merely browsing, and went on to the final brothel.

There the story remained the same. Lots of the ladies of the best saloon in Eagle Pass, but no sign of his wife. After remaining long enough to allay any suspicions, he departed for the hotel. He arrived only minutes after Eli had dressed, seen his most entertaining visitor to the side entrance of the livery, and hurried to their appointment.

"She's not there. Can't find Amy anywhere," Ezekiel complained.

"You saw all of the girls at each bordello?"

"Yes. All those who weren't . . . working."

Eli didn't like to rub the obvious in his friend's face, but someone had to. "There's your answer. She was, ah, otherwise occupied."

"Damn the fatherless wretch who was with her then!" Ezekiel snarled. "I'll cut off his balls and feed them to him for breakfast."

"Easy, easy, ole friend. That's hardly turning the other cheek, is it?"

Ezekial scowled. "She's my wife! What am I supposed to do? What am I expected to feel? I want a slow death by torture for Weatherby when the time comes."

"All well and good, Zeke. And maybe you can have your wish. For the time being, though, go back tomorrow and try again. There's too much at stake now for you to lose control and expose our purpose."

"All right, Eli. Have it your way. I suppose I did get a bit too hot under the collar."

Early the next evening, Ezekiel entered the first of Weatherby's whorehouses nearly to collide with his wife. He almost let the whole plan explode by calling her name, only to catch himself in time and make a more expected remark.

"Now here's a charming piece I didn't see yesterday. What a divine figure. Such a compelling set of eyes. I think I should like to entertain you a bit tonight, my dear."

"Why thank you, sir. You are a forceful and intriguing man, I must say."

"Madam Pearl, here is the direction given me by Captain Weatherby. Observe that it says, 'sample, inspect and otherwise make use of.' That applies in this instance. I wish the services of this beauty for the night. Perhaps I shall require her to grace my modest quarters when the new church is built. For now, come, my dove. We will away to our trysting spot."

"My room is at the top of the stairs, all the way back over the alley," Amy told him lifelessly, trying to hide the pounding excitement of her heart.

Inside the small cubicle, Amy flung herself into the strong, protective arms of her husband and wept wildly for several long minutes. He stroked her hair and forehead and kissed away the worry lines. At last she subsided to tiny whimpers, and he pushed her away for a moment. With a glow of tenderest love, he examined her and then drew her close again.

"Oh, I feared I had lost you forever," Amy sobbed.

"I know, I know," Ezekiel told her. "My dearest, nothing could keep me from your rescue."

"But . . . the danger. If Captain Weatherby finds out—"

Ezekiel raised a hand. "None of that. Eli is here with me. We have only to devise a means of attacking from within, time it for when the cavalry arrives, and then deliver the decisive blow. Soon you and all the girls will be free. I am deeply wounded at the pitiful sight of those poor, confused Sioux girls, and many show signs of beatings. All have been poorly fed. Even Sylvia and some of your friends from Eagle Pass look a lot worse for wear."

"It is awful. But now, come sit by me on the bed. I have to tell you about what happened." Patiently, as though explaining to a small child, Amy told Ezekiel of her capture, the men she had been forced to service in every intimate manner, and her terrible days since coming to Breakneck Gap.

He held her tight and kissed away each new flood of tears. "It doesn't matter. None of it matters now, my darling. I have you back, and soon we will be away from here," he told her. "On bended knee I swear my undying love for you, no matter how many men you have entertained in the past, present, or future. All you must keep in your mind is that you are mine, and I am going to save you from this hideous town. 'Vengeance is mine, sayeth the Lord', and this time He's going to get a little help from Eli Holten and me."

Chapter 14

How deeply the ache ran within him, Kicking Elk thought as he stared across the distance toward the whiteman village in the valley. What was one white woman to the will of the Great Spirit? The Sun Dance must be held in this place. The ones who had come to their village and stolen away the yellow-haired one had brought her here. Somewhere, over there, beyond his ability to see details, she lived, slept, ate . . . and she would be there when the combined force of all the Dakota attacked.

Perhaps she would die. *His* Ra-shell die? Kicking Elk grunted impatiently, disgusted at the way his thoughts ran, yet unable to dismiss them. Yes, Ra-shell would die, if the Great Spirit wanted it that way. Pain began again as he contemplated this. Stone Heart edged closer and spoke in a low whisper, his tone critical, demanding.

"We should not be here. It is not the time to attack against the medicine guns. Let us give the word. Start the raids. Kill the white men. Steal their stock and burn their lodges. It must be done while the young men are still fiery in their anger."

Kicking Elk made an impatient gesture. "We have

talked of this before. It *is* the time to attack. Here is where the Great Spirit wants us to erect the Sun Dance lodge and raise the great pole. The badmen who come and go from this place still prey upon our people in their lodges. Let this build in the fighting men a white heat of anger. You forget, my friend, that our goal is not merely to kill the white man. We must clean the filth from the sacred soil of this valley.

"We'll bring the pressure directly on the white man's village. Our *tonweyapi* have been watching. The evil men come and go. Some to attack our people. Most do harm to their own kind. Take cattle, take from places the *wasicun* call banks. They come back to drink whiskey, make songs. This is why the village is here. If we kill these men who come here, close off the town from all, then attack, we will win."

"But the council—" Stone Heart began, appealing to the decisions reached over the previous days.

"Raids on other whites, even the pony-soldiers, are to be planned, but not done until after we weaken this place. If the pony-soldiers do not come to do it, we must. If we fail here, then all whites will suffer. This village must fall."

Stone Heart nodded in agreement, though he didn't approve. Where was the honor to be gained in closing off the narrow gap that led to the valley? Glory came in battle, not sitting behind rocks and chasing away a few white men who tried to go past. Patiently he put his objections in words.

"Don't worry, old friend," Kicking Elk told him, one hand on the warrior's shoulder. "There will be plenty of glory when we ride in among the lodges in this valley to burn and kill."

In his boyhood, Eli Holten had read many stories about men and the sea. He had also heard the tales told by those who had challenged the mighty oceans. Making love with Marilee Weatherby, he compared it with the gentle sway of a ship on the high seas, headed into the teeth of a tremendous storm. At first there came the unnatural calm. A gentle rocking, dipping motion, made suddenly exciting by tentative explorations, like gusts that billowed out ahead of the squall line. Then, as the tempo built, the sun would be blotted out, and the winds build to gale force.

The sea swelled, and whitecaps flecked the heaving rollers. Water burst across the deck of his imagined ship as the hay started to fly in the loft where Marilee always met Eli for their afternoons of secret romance. With fevered speed the tempest grew into a powerful hurricane, only to subside with whimpers and moans as the peaceful eye drew near.

With happy sounds and soft touches, the genteel English girl collapsed on Holten's chest. Her powerful muscles kept his mighty phallus tightly clasped deep inside her tingling passage. Spent, though still wildly stimulated, the long, arched shaft pulsated with the inner rhythm of his delightful partner. Immobilized by their efforts, it seemed nothing could stir them.

Then, like the feared far side of the hurricane, passions whipped to a boil again. And again. The hours whisked away in a heady mingling of their spirits. Body melded into body, and soul into soul. Finally, oblivious to an appreciative, unseen audience below, the girl's energies were spent. When the talking started, Miles Tate and Jimmy Barkley slipped quietly outside the livery, certain that their afternoon's entertainment had ended.

"You've been here four days now," Marilee began as she lay in Holten's arms. He idly teased one of her pert nipples until it slowly began to harden with a memory of desire.

"And we've made love up here every one of them," Eli told her.

"How happy I've been," she sighed out heavily. "Yes, I'm quite pleased with the arrangement. And I've decided that you will do nicely."

"How's that? Do for what?"

Marilee raised herself on one elbow and gazed intently into the scout's deep gray eyes. "Eli, I hope not to offend you by telling you this. It should have been obvious I wasn't a virgin."

"Of course. What has that to do with you and me?"

"You, Eli, are the first man ever to best my father in bed."

"What!" Caught entirely off guard by this casual revelation, Holten recoiled slightly, his eyes wide.

"Please. You must understand, Eli. We were on the high seas when my mother died. The Civil War was still raging in your country. Only months left to the end, but all the same hostilities continued."

"But I thought your father commanded a man-o'-war in the Royal Navy," Eli managed to get out in an attempt at denial of what Marilee said.

"He did. During peacetime—and your Civil War was peacetime for England—the captain of a Royal Navy ship of the line could bring his wife and older children along. Oh, it was frowned on, you can be sure. But when a ship's mission might last anywhere from two to seven years, the Admiralty would allow it on the quiet, you see. Anyway, let me get on with it. I was nearly eleven when my mother died. Father had this one last assignment. It was to bring supplies to the Confederate States.

"Naturally, he could not put into port and let me off the ship. He dearly loved me, and I him. Too, he missed Mother sorely. I wanted to do something for him. To make him happy again. I don't recall who it was that suggested it the first time. Actually, I think it was he, although I certainly made it clear, in the privacy of the captain's cabin, that I would not turn away such attentions. Following the first time, after I learned how much pleasure it gave me, as well as him, I frequently sought him out."

"Marilee, this — this must be painful for you."

"No. Not at all. Within a month, Father would use me as a wife nearly every night, while he continued to cherish me as a daughter. He does so to this day. I'm the only woman in his life. When we began, I was so young and ignorant. I didn't fully understand the implications until we had to abandon the ship and came to live in this country. We settled in Texas for a while. I was precocious, and I truly relished having sex. I slept with many men and boys I thought might be able to match Father's prowess. None did, until you."

"That's quite flattering, Marilee. But what are you driving at with this awful confession?" Real concern for her sensibilities and well-being colored the scout's words.

"I have no regrets about my relationship with my father. It's his other activities that disturb me. Over the years, he has been obsessed with the idea of building a small empire somewhere. When he settled in this valley,

I thought he might have what he wanted at little or no cost. Now I realize that he poses too great a threat to far too many lives.

"The killing started with the aborigines. Then your army came." Marilee's face blanched. "All that bloodshed! It was all I could do to keep my revulsion from being apparent to Father. Yet I love him and don't want to see him hurt. Even so, I feel—no, I know that he must be stopped. I'd like to see to it that he is. Oh, I still cherish him. And I sleep with him. But he must be shown his error. It's going to take some time, but I believe my father can be beaten. Will—will you promise to be the one to do it?"

"You, ah, leave me with a lot of unanswered questions," Holten delayed. "What makes you feel I'm the right one?"

"You are brave, resourceful, and determined. You have to be here to bring about his defeat as it is. All I ask is that you do so as one who could possibly take his place in my life." Marilee ended with a shy, weakening smile.

"You're right, Marilee," Eli told her softly. "I'm here to do it, no matter what. And I agree. Your father can be beaten."

"Darling, there's so much to go over," Amy told her husband as they entered her room at the brothel. "Your being here has meant a lot to the girls. Now they have definite hope. Do you know when the Army will be back?"

"No, Amy. I do not. Nor does Eli. Now tell me everything. Take your time, and make sure you leave nothing out."

Amy thought a moment, composing her hard-gained information into some sort of order. "First off, as I said, the girls have hope now. They see your coming here as a guarantee of being rescued. Now, that big brick building is the center of everything. That's an armory of some sort. The big guns are kept there."

"That much we already know. But don't leave anything out because you think it is too obvious, honey," Ezekiel returned.

Amy continued, giving details about the sentries on the roof of the structure, the number and location of most of the men, and something of their apparent abilities. When she finished, Ezekiel Smith sat in contemplative silence for a long while.

"One of the big guns is not at the armory any longer. Do you have any idea where it might have been taken?"

"Oh, yes. That. The day before you got here, Captain Weatherby ordered it taken outside town and set up in a hidden spot. I don't have any idea where."

Ezekiel patted his wife's hand. "You've done well, dear. Better than most could under the circumstances."

Despite the danger, no matter the terrible surroundings and strain of the past days, they could forestall their emotions no longer. Ezekiel took Amy in his arms and held her tightly. He kissed her hair, forehead, ears, eyes, cheeks, and lips. When they broke for a much-needed gulp of air, Ezekiel held her at arm's length.

He carefully examined each contour of her exquisite body and felt again the warm flush that pleasure brought to him. Hesitantly, from an innate shyness with women, Ezekiel reached out and cupped one firm, full breast. His eyes shined with happiness, and his face relaxed fully for the first time since he had learned of his wife's capture. Then, following his thoughts at the moment, his forehead creased again in concern.

"I know . . . that is, I'd understand it, under the circumstances, you wouldn't want . . . to—"

"Oh, but I do, darling. I surely do want to make love with you. Come to me, husband, and give me your all."

Rising, Amy began to slide out of her clothing.

Eli Holten met the Reverend Ezekiel Smith late that afternoon at the *Swan and Crown* saloon. They sat at a far table, drinking from huge schooners of beer. Ezekiel had most of the news.

"According to Amy," Ezekiel began after the preliminaries had been disposed of, "the gun crews sleep in the magazine, alongside their weapons. Have hammocks slung there most of the time. Rifles, shotguns, and revolvers belonging to everyone in town are kept in racks on the second floor. Powder is in a vault in the basement of the tower. At the present time there are forty-one men with fighting ability in town. That's not counting two boys of eleven who serve in the magazine as powder monkeys, Mr. Tandy, who's thirteen and rated as a midshipman, and the captain. Then there's Mr. Yardley, the First Officer, Mr. Biggs, Second Officer, the bartenders in the saloons—there's five of them in each—and the bouncers in the whorehouses, who make another dozen."

"Quite a little army Weatherby's gathered," Eli observed, impressed. "Talk is that no one is getting in or out of town. The Sioux have closed off the Gap."

The reverend contemplated that. "Hummm. That could cause complications. Now then, as to the missing gun. Amy says that it was taken out of town the day before we got here. To be hidden somewhere. Only no one she's talked to knows the location, or at least isn't saying."

"That won't be too hard to find. We can always use the excuse of selecting lodge pole pines for our church," the scout replied. "I got a pair of converts lined up this morning. Caught 'em sufferin' from too much 'night before.' Told 'em that some bodacious praying would cure a hangover. We can take them out and look around tomorrow."

"I can't come along. When I got back to my hotel room, I found a message waiting from the captain. My, ah, new 'mistress' and I are to dine tomorrow at noon with the captain and Miss Weatherby."

"Coming up in the social order, aren't you?" Eli teased. Then he turned serious. "We have to spike those guns before the cavalry rides in here to take the town. Without that, it will be impossible. Like the first time. With them separated, it's going to be hard to do. If we locate that gun tomorrow, we'll have to leave it alone. I'll let you know where it is. Also, tell the Thunder Saloon girls to keep at it. We can use all the information they can get. Once we've gathered all the intelligence we can, it looks like the best bet is for me to slip out of here and go find the regiment.

"It will be up to you and the girls to spike the guns. Oh, and there's one little thing that might play right to help us. Marilee Weatherby thinks her father is off his rail. She'll do what she can to help stop him."

Ezekiel whistled tunelessly. "After you've left, how do I let her know it's time to do something?"

"It'll have to be handled through me. She, ah, trusts

me entirely in this thing."

"Uh-huh. From that cat-and-canary grin, I know exactly which big argument you used to convince her," Ezekiel fired back, with a nod toward a spot below the scout's belt.

Rachel Johnson continued to gather all the information she could. She pretended delight at the unusual way that some of the gun crewmen preferred to avail themselves of her services. Although it made her backside sore, she also knew it pleased them, which in turn made them talkative. The majority who adhered to this form had spent years at sea in the Royal Navy, "Reaming out the ship's boys, don't ye know."

For all her worldliness and sexual freedom, *that* revelation disgusted and shocked Rachel. Still, she strove to empty them of every shred of knowledge that would make her exposé into an explosive piece. Hidden between her thin mattress and the springs, the pile of notes grew. At supper, four nights after the preachers rode in, Rachel met a young woman she had not seen before. She soon realized that this competent female could be an even greater source of facts.

"I'm so glad I met you, Amy," Rachel gushed after the pair had finished their bland meal.

"There's someone here you must meet," Amy returned. "He's not really what he seems to be. He calls himself Deacon Jones now. Came in with the traveling minister. Well, the minister is my husband, and his so-called assistant is really Eli Holten, Chie—"

"Chief Scout for the Twelfth Cavalry," Rachel finished.

Surprise lighted Amy's eyes. "You know him?"

"Do I? Sister, I know him better than his own mother. I was with the Twelfth on their way here," she exaggerated, "when the Sioux grabbed me. I learned a lot while I was in their camp, I can tell you. What a story it will make!" she enthused. "John Morrison is going to become the most famous newspaperman of our times."

Unsure of what Rachel babbled about, Amy smiled vacantly. "I'm sure he will, dear. Now, we must meet with Eli tonight. Tell him everything you've learned since being taken by the Sioux up to this evening."

"Sure. Sure. Where do we meet?"

"I'll come to your room and let you know."

They met an hour after sundown, behind the large outhouse that sat in back of the brothel where Rachel had been confined. Of the three of them, she had the least freedom of movement. She openly showed her joy at being reunited with the scout.

When the hugging and kissing ended, Rachel stepped back and uttered a small, contented sigh. "Now, I'm going to have to interview you to fill in the blank spaces in what happened elsewhere after the Sioux captured me."

"No, Rachel. It's me who wants to interview you. Tell me about your experience with the Sioux. Was it the Sans Arc?"

"They called themselves the *Itazipicola*."

"That's the Sans Arc, all right. It means 'without bows.' Who was their leader?"

"Oh, yes. I got to know him rather, ah, well. He called himself *Hehaka Cankpe-e*."

"Kicking Elk," Eli translated coldly.

"He held a big council. Talked to all the others. I picked up a lot of their language, but I couldn't understand all of what they said. Something about killing a lot of whites. About this place being bad, and how the army had failed to throw out the white men here."

Holten needed only a minute's thought to realize what Rachel had overheard. If the Army failed a second time, or didn't try to removed Weatherby and his frontier scum, then a general uprising would be called for. Worse, since it seemed that the Sioux had not waited for the Army to try and had started a blockade of their own, it was probably too late to stop a wave of bloodshed.

Chapter 15

At the head of the snowy linen-covered table, Capt. William C. Weatherby tinkled a small pewter bell. Immediately, servants began to bring in silver trays from the kitchen. The first bore a large tureen of chicken soup, the broth crystal clear, containing bits of carrot, turnip, onion and cattail root, with plentiful shreds of light and dark meat. The second contained sliced loaves of fresh-baked bread, wedges of cheese, and a pot of Scottish marmalade. Behind came a roast of venison leg, peas, potatoes, corn, and a gravy boat of horseradish sauce.

"A simple repast, if I may say so," the Captain announced to his guests. "Though it would be a bit more traditional with some good English mutton."

Seated around the table, Ezekiel Smith and his wife, Amy, shared space with Marilee Weatherby and her father. Sight of the heavy meal made them groan inwardly. More, they knew, would be following. Weatherby had promised a surprise for later. Ezekiel wondered if it would be gastronomical or of some other variety.

"Have you ever been in Eagle Pass, Reverend Piker?" Weatherby inquired.

The unexpected question, presented so casually, almost made Ezekiel choke on his soup. He sputtered, coughed, and at last controlled the spasm.

"Uh, no. Not at all. Small place, I hear."

"Oh, well, no matter that. It is small. I have a special mission I would like you to perform, and figured that if you were familiar with the town and its people, it would make your task simpler."

"What is that, sir?"

"Oh, it's a part of my surprise. You'll learn all about it over brandy and cigars. Now, enjoy the soup."

Subdued and somewhat suspicious, Ezekiel and Amy went back to their plates. Heavy silver service clicked musically against bone-thin Wexford china. Captain Weatherby finished his serving, belched appreciatively, and started on the venison.

"I'm really inordinately pleased with the way things have gone here, you know?"

"You have accomplished a lot," Ezekiel had to admit.

"Seven buildings is hardly a metropolis. Yet it represents a positive step forward. My greatest contribution, however, has been to my fellow man." Weatherby waved his hand and arm in an expansive gesture that took in all of Breakneck Gap. "Most of these men were nothing but riff-raff and rabble before we came here. They had nothing, no standing, no goals, no future. Now . . ."

Carried away by his own vision of his achievements, Weatherby began to wave about a hinged leg joint. "They have their proper station in life, the lowly serving the needs and pleasures of the educated and elite. I want to say again how grateful I am for your coming here, reverend.

"Religion is a useful tool for manipulating the masses

to accept their lot in life and to keep them from striving to improve it. Heaven forbid if these louts could ever rise above their natural station! But, praise be, a good dose of Bible quotations can always keep them content. Has there ever been a religion created by a poor man?

"Of course not," Weatherby answered his own question. "Baseness is all that can come out of being base. Rich men dictate the content of religious belief to other rich men, who in turn sell it to the poor as a panacea for their woes. Now that's where it all ends up. Eh? Don't you agree, reverend? Eh what?"

Throughout the little dissertation, Ezekiel Smith had found it necessary to bite his tongue to keep from making thunderous reply. Now, with the opportunity open, his ministerial soul cried out to blast this heretic into the darkest, hottest corner of Hell. Good sense and a built-in caution prevented the fiery outburst he had first framed.

"Right you are, captain. You have an astute and remarkable mind. Now, my curiosity is beginning to overwhelm me. What is this surprise you promised, and what is the special assignment you hinted at?"

"All in due time, sir. All in due . . . ah, yes. Must be a sign of approaching age when one begins to pontificate. We've a fine ham, with wild onions, beans, and yams next course. Good white wine to go with it, too. By the way, this is excellent claret, is it not?"

"How did you get it out here?"

"Sent for it, of course. Costly, but worth it. Men of quality must maintain certain standards, eh? Of course they must. This is the place to grow in, reverend. Your church can prosper here."

"Glad you feel that way about it, Captain. So long as

there is a profit in it — and I don't mean my namesake the prophet — I'm your man."

Weatherby condescended to chuckle at the reverend's poor pun. "It's time for my little surprise and your mission, if you're willing to undertake it."

Weatherby lifted the small bell once more and gave it a brief shake. A man in butler's uniform answered.

"Send the child in now, Roberts."

"Yes, sir."

A few moments later, the servant returned with Elizabeth Brewster in tow. Ezekiel Smith had been aware that the girl had accompanied the soiled doves of the Thunder Saloon. He had expected the worst, only to discover she was not employed in any of the bordellos. Now Captain Weatherby answered his curiosity.

"This young lady came here by mistake. Her name is Elizabeth Brewster, and she's the daughter of a federal judge. At present the family makes its home in Eagle Pass. It has been my intention to see her reunited with them. Your timely arrival, reverend, has provided a convenient solution to my problem.

"I think it would be entirely proper and fitting if you were to be her escort back to, ah, civilization." Weatherby beamed over the scene, basking in the warm glow of his own brilliance.

Elizabeth, on the other hand, had not been prepared for this surprise reunion with the Reverend Ezekiel Smith. Her eyes widened and she made small, fluttery gestures with her hands. Impulsively she took a step forward as she spoke.

"I see you have found your wife and rescued her from that den of iniquity, Reverend Smith," Elizabeth said sweetly. Then her natural spite and self-righteousness bubbled over. "Of course, you needn't have worried. She was quite at home with the rest of the prostitutes."

"Elizabeth!" Amy exclaimed. "The shock of coming here must have affected you, child. You're confused. *This is the Reverend Piker*, dear. Not my husband."

"Wh-why, yes," Ezekiel stammered. He turned in appeal to the suddenly stony-faced Weatherby. "I've never seen this child before. Something must have happened to addle her thinking."

"Oh, there's nothing wrong with me, Mrs. Smith, reverend." Elizabeth turned to the captain. "He has a church in Eagle Pass. It's not a very good one, though. He allows *whores* to attend. He even married one."

"You're positive of this, child?"

"Yes, Captain Weatherby," Elizabeth returned in dulcet tones.

"The child's lying," Amy hastened to say.

"That's enough," Weatherby snapped. He grabbed up the pewter bell and shook it furiously. When the butler and another burly servant arrived, the captain pointed to Ezekiel.

"Hold this man for me. And send someone for his assistant. I must make further inquiries into this matter."

Ezekiel tried to bluster. "Now see here —"

His protests cut off when the butler hit him behind the ear with a shot-filled cosh.

"Oh my, Father!" Marilee exclaimed as she came to her feet. "Such shocking revelations. I'm afraid it is a bit too much for me. Do I have your permission to retire?"

"Yes, of course, my child."

"There's something else, captain," Elizabeth offered, eyes aglow.

"What might be troubling you, dear Elizabeth?"

161

She still felt the warm tingle in that place at the juncture of her thighs. Only moments before the summons came to visit the captain's table, she had been in the arms of Geoffrey Tandy. Great shivers of pleasure had coursed through her as he drove his slim, rigid instrument deep within her receptive body. Several times each day, over the past four, they had managed to experiment further into the delights of love. Only her fear of becoming with child — he seemed to have a most copious and endless supply of sap — had decided her to end their relationship.

When she proposed it to Geoffrey, he had made light of the possibility. Utterly infatuated with and enslaved by Elizabeth, he could not bring himself to think of abandoning their wonderful trysts. It was then that she determined to bring the affair to the attention of Captain Weatherby.

"I — I'm terribly sorry to have to say this. I mean, Geoffrey is really a dear, sweet boy and all. Only — "

A crafty light emanated from Elizabeth's eyes. Her face had undergone a transformation, like that of a skilled actress. Amy spotted it in an instant. Aware of the amorous entanglement of the two youngsters, she suddenly visualized what Elizabeth might plan to reveal. Before she could speak, the damage was done.

"He — well, he forced himself upon me. I tried to prevent it, but — oh, captain, he has stolen away my innocence!"

"You vicious, lying bitch!" Amy shrieked. She started at the scheming girl with clawed talons, only to be restrained by two servants who had also rushed into the room.

"Tut-tut, Mrs., ah, Smith. One in your position

really shouldn't criticize. After all, whom should I believe? This horribly wronged child, or a prostitute, whose husband has invaded my domain for one nefarious purpose or another?" Weatherby summoned additional assistance.

"Take this woman back to the brothel. Have her properly disciplined. And send someone for Mister Tandy. He is to be confined with the spurious Reverend Piker until he is hanged for rape."

Gunfire erupted from inside the Homestead State Bank. As the town marshal rushed in that direction, shotgun in hand, more shots sounded from the Lawson Valley Bank a block away in the opposite direction.

"Goddammit!" the lawman exploded aloud. "Ain't never had a robbery in Merriman. Now two banks get hit at the same time."

Although small, Merriman, Nebraska, boasted two prosperous banks, four blocks of business district, and a growing population, added to that night by the wife of the marshal, who had produced a fine, healthy, eight-pound baby boy. Marshal Hinton had been up most of the night and, with only two hours' sleep, his eyes felt gritty. He had started for the Homestead, so he continued in that direction. Grimly he wondered what he would find.

Inside, the bank looked like a slaughterhouse.

Sprays of blood smeared the walls. Three corpses lay sprawled behind the tellers' cages, limbs grotesque in the postures of death. A woman crouched in one corner, wailing in horror. A small child huddled beside her, bawling hysterically. Five lean, hard men, sixguns held ready, stood over the cowed occupants.

"Keep scoopin' out that money, banker," Pete Miller growled as he menaced the bank president with a cocked Colt.

"I-I-I'm moving as fast as I can," the portly, balding man stammered.

"Then slow down, dammit. You're spillin' some."

Suddenly the crying boy darted away from his frightened mother. He made three steps toward the door when Pete Miller turned slightly, his attention leaving the bank president. In a blur of motion, Pete swung his Colt and squeezed the trigger.

Two hundred fifty grains of lead turned the young lad's head into mush. His eyes bulged as he skidded on his heels toward the front wall. Howling in anguish, his mother leaped up and raced toward him. Buck Nelson, at the door, blasted her into oblivion with a round from his Winchester. Made uneasy by the sudden disturbance, Buck pulled back the green blind and glanced through the glass partition at the boardwalk and beyond.

Out in the dusty street, the lookout and horse-holder spotted Marshal Hinton a moment before the lawdog saw him. His advantage did him little good, though. A tight shot column of double-aught made a mangled red mess of his chest as the marshal opened up with one barrel of the L. C. Smith ten-gauge he carried.

Spun away from the skitterish horses, the dying man barely managed to retain his hold. The doors flew open in the next second, and five outlaws spilled out onto the boardwalk. Pete Miller brought up the rear. When the scattergun bellowed once more, another load of buckshot drove Buck Nelson back into his boss. Two pellets bit flesh on Pete's shoulder and earlobe, and a hot trickle of blood ran down his neck. Calm in the face of sure death, Pete raised on tiptoes and squeezed off a shot at the marshal.

Hot lead from a Colt .45 made a widow of Mrs. Hinton and an orphan of newly born Jamie.

Across the street, by the general mercantile, two barefoot boys hooted in excitement at the bloody action going on around them. One of the bandits raised his Remington and put a bullet through the breastbone of the nearest youngster.

The little redhead dropped without a sound. His friend screamed in terror and began to run down the street. Calmly, with evil deliberation, another masked stickup artist took careful aim on the fleeing boy. He fired his Connecticut Arms Bulldog, and the .44 slug sped on its way.

It struck the running lad between his shoulder blades and erupted out the front in a welter of crimson gore. Dead before he hit the dusty ground, the child's scream cut off to leave an eerie silence. Two more shots came from inside the Lawson Valley Bank.

Then five hardcases tumbled out through the door and leaped astride their rearing mounts. Spurs flashed, and the horses dug in their hind haunches. In a shower of dust, they pelted down the street to where the rest of the gang waited.

"Keep together, boys," Pete Miller commanded. "We're headin' North."

Already, the citizens of Merriman had begun to rally. Rifles and shotguns blasted out at the robbers from several store fronts and a second-story window of the small hotel. No resistance came from either bank. Everyone inside the two establishments had been ruthlessly shot to death. "Leave no witnesses," was Pete Miller's motto.

In her room, oblivious of the disaster to their escape plans, Rachel Johnson busily scribbled away on the latest installment in the fanciful article she was composing for the *Boston Herald*. Her prose grew more flowery and her personal participation more swashbuckling with each line.

Now that agents of the Army have slipped into this evil nest of bandits, the end is only a matter of hours away. With your fearless correspondent, John Morrison of the Boston Herald, *leading the way, the friendly spies soon discovered the defenses and weaknesses of the English invasion force. At the insistence of the Army, this reporter has organized the women being held against their will, so that they are working toward a common goal with the heroic Army volunteers who have infiltrated the community. In a confidential remark, Chief Scout Eli Holten revealed that in General Corrington's opinion, without the invaluable assistance of this* Boston Herald *reporter, the expedition would have been lost.*

A moment later, the door burst open. "Okay, honey. Off yer belly and spread them legs. You've got another buffala hunter to fuck," the madam cackled.

Rachel quickly hid her notes and rolled over. She smiled invitingly and pulled loose the filmy dressing gown that barely covered her body. Her guest already had his long, swollen penis in his hand.

As he watched her many and ample treasures revealed, he began to rapidly stroke his staff and sidled over to the bed.

"We'uns is gonna have us some fun, boy-howdy!" he bellowed.

His breath stank of stale whiskey and strong tobacco,

and it made Rachel's stomach roil. Oh, well, she consoled herself. Anything for the cause.

While the slender, lengthy phallus slid up and down in Rachel's always-ready cavern, her mind left reality to compose greater fantasy.

This reporter, assisting the powers of goodness and defending the rights of the little man, in the finest tradition — "Oh! Aaaah! More! More! Harder-deeper-faster! That's . . . it . . . that's . . . IT!" — *of American journalism* . . .

Chapter 16

Captain William Weatherby's zealous followers had added a bit of dressing to the order to confine Ezekiel Smith. Punches and kicks had been delivered in liberal quantities before the unconscious man had been hurled into a sturdy, thick-walled, windowless room behind the largest saloon.

The structure, the minister realized soon after he regained consciousness, was one of Weatherby's more intelligent innovations, an ice house. It was nearly full of the great blocks now, and he had only their frigid bulk and piles of sawdust for company. A quick inspection of the interior verified to him the hopelessness of any attempt to escape by digging or prying his way out. Twenty minutes after his confinement, the bolt rattled on the opposite side of the door.

When it flew open, two burly gunners threw in the bruised and bloody form of a small boy. Ezekiel caught the lad and steadied him, easing the limp figure to the floorboards of the ice room.

"Bloody two of a kind, you ask me," one gunner voiced his opinion. "Sneaks and cheats."

Ezekiel knelt beside the sobbing boy after the door closed. "I couldn't . . . help . . . it. She . . . even—even asked to —"

"Asked what, son?" the preacher inquired.

"Asked for us to . . . well . . . to, ah, get into bed together."

"Who is this she?" Ezekiel inquired. Unconscious during Elizabeth's betrayal, he had no idea of what had happened.

"Elizabeth Brewster, sir. She fixed it up so I could see her alone of afternoons. Then she began kissing me and squeezing my, ah, privates, sir. Said she wanted no one but me. She begged me, sir. Begged to make what she called mad, passionate love."

"Elizabeth Brewster?" Ezekiel repeated in disbelief. "I — I hardly expected to encounter such a situation. Not with Elizabeth Brewster."

"All the same, sir," Geoffrey Tandy went on as he dried his eyes. "That's what happened. Before I knew it, she had my pecker up right smart and we was rolling around in the bed. Eager though she was, she didn't know a thing about it and," a note of returning pride crept into the lad's voice, "I had to teach her."

"I . . . see. Now then, you are young Mr. Tandy, right?"

"Yes, sir. Most people, other than the officers, call me Geoffrey."

"All right, Geoffrey. I'm Reverend Smith, but my friends call me Zeke. Now, what can you tell me about this place we're in?"

"Even when there's ice in it, like now, sir, they use it for a brig. I've seen blokes fearsome cold and stiff from bein' here for a couple of days. There's no way out, 'cept the door. Always two guards. Sometimes more than that, if there's a couple of drunks or the sort that want

169

handling."

"What do they plan to do to us?"

Geoffrey looked down at the floor and his smooth, youthful skin paled. "Me, they're gonna hang. You . . . well, they might allow you a firing squad. You see, to Cap'n Weatherby, rape is a far worse crime than what you did."

"Rape? I thought you said Elizabeth wanted you to do it?"

"Oh, she did, Reverend Zeke. Only, well, she told the captain a far different story."

"And you have no right to have your side heard?"

"Oh, no, sir. Who'd believe me, anyway? The gunners, that lot which sailed with the Captain in old times at least, say that a stiff prick has no conscience. It don't know rape from a romp with a doxy, nor male from female, when it's in need. For my own part, I don't believe that."

"Nor I. Man has choice. You need an attorney."

"An advocate, you mean?"

"Yes. I shall demand of the Captain that you are provided with counsel."

"Won't do no good. You're a condemned man, too, Reverend Zeke."

His gorge risen by this injustice, Reverend Ezekiel Smith strode to the door and began to pound. "You out there! Listen to me, you men! I am a minister of the Gospel. I demand to speak with Captain Weatherby about this horrid injustice to the boy. I must see him now. Do you hear me?"

A two-day hard ride brought the fleeing desperadoes to the fringes of the Black Hills. Pete Miller and his men

170

had sustained no further losses and felt confident they had left the last posse far behind. They carried with them some thirty-five thousand dollars in gold and silver coin and paper money. Despite the circuitous route selected, Pete had a destination in mind.

During the week when he planned the robberies of the banks in Merriman, he had learned of an owlhoot refuge deep in the dark, brooding mountains. Breakneck Gap was reputed to be the sort of place he and the boys could hole up in until things cooled off. They had come this far, and Pete grew more confident that he had made the right decision with each mile that sped by under their cantering mounts.

Shortly before mid-morning he had spotted the first of the landmarks that his contact had given him to guide the gang to their secure hiding place. More hours translated into miles, and Pete spotted the next guideposts. By a bit past noon, they had gained some eight hundred feet in altitude and started into the backslopes of the south-facing Black Hills.

"You sure we're going' the right way?" Barry Howard asked his boss.

"According to the directions I got," Pete answered back.

"Sure hope they got lots of whiskey in that place," the rat-faced Barry declared wistfully.

"I thought you were death on booze," Pete responded.

"Oh, I am. But I always like a few shots after killin' women and kids," the curly blond outlaw explained. "That little bit shouldn't keep me out of Heaven."

When the sun showed a noticeable slant down the western sky, near three in the afternoon, Pete located the final landmark, the tall, circular ridge of rugged stone and broken earth that marked the protective wall of the valley. He signaled for a halt and reined in with the rest of his boys.

"There she is. My bet's an hour from now we'll be bellied up to the bar, washin' the trail dust out of our mouths." The gang gave off a ragged cheer.

Pete lost his bet.

Before they reached the dark slash that marked the passage through the gap, Pete Miller and his gang met Kicking Elk of the Sans Arc Sioux.

With a suddenness that none of the gang had witnessed before, warriors rose out of the tall buffalo grass and swung onto the backs of their snorting, prancing mounts. The maneuver put the gang inside a closed circle of rifles and bows. Directly ahead, Pete saw an intricately costumed Indian, astride a magnificent stallion. His full war bonnet waved gently in the light breeze, more feathers rippled along the decorated shaft of a long lance, and six dangled from the lower rim and three points on the face of a bullhide shield. And such elaborate ornamentation had not been confined to the man.

His mount had feathers braided into his mane and tied-up tail, and two, in a beaded purse, dangled from the hackamore bridle. The big animal flared its nostrils and pranced impatiently. The brave on its back urged it forward with his knees. Kicking Elk raised his lance high over his head and curvetted his war pony in front of the circle of his followers. After a dozen intricate dance-like steps to left and right, the *otancan* wheeled to face the shocked whites.

"*Hu ihpeya wicayapo!*" he shouted defiantly.

"What the hell did he say?" Pete asked of his men.

Barry Howard spoke up. "Says they are gonna grab

172

us and kill us and fuck us in the ass."

"In that order?"

"Not necessarily."

Arrogantly, his hawk-beak nose cut the air as Kicking Elk turned his head to examine each of Miller's robbers with contempt. With equal panache, he dismounted by swinging his left leg over his pony's neck and sliding to the ground. He took three steps forward and pulled free both flaps of his loincloth. He adjusted their length through the back of the girdle at his waist. Then he laid the matched ends on the ground and lifted his lance, point down. This he drove through the tanned and decorated elk hide, pinning himself in place. He straightened and reached out. Stone Heart tossed Kicking Elk his shiny new Winchester repeater.

"*Maka kin le, mitawa ca!*" he yelled at Pete and the gang.

"Says, 'I own the earth.' What he means is, he ain't gonna move from there until the fight's over or he's dead."

"Angry feller," Pete observed, hoping his light words would ease the tension of his men. There were far too many Indians out there to suit him.

Warcries burst from every savage throat as the Sioux urged their horses forward and charged down on the helpless men. Typically of Indian combat, the warriors fired individually, as the Spirit moved them, most aimed far above their targets. For their part, Pete Miller and his gang had no such handicap.

"Dismount and pour it on, boys. They're gonna try to ride us over. If we get through that, we hit the saddle again and streak for that pass."

Using their prone horses for parapets, the outlaws began an accurate and effective fire. First one, then three more warriors spun off their churning ponies and fell into the grass, staining it with gouts of their blood. Bullets cracked through the air around the attackers but, as they drew nearer, the majority loosed a flight of arrows.

Feathered shafts slammed into the ground. One horse screamed with agony as two missiles pierced its neck. To Pete's left a man cried out and rolled on his side, drawn in a foetal ball around the quivering shaft that protruded from his chest. Then the wall of horsemen hit the hasty defenses.

Stone warclubs whirred through the air. Meaty smacks followed where they touched flesh. Outlaws and Indians cried out in pain, and in a flash the pounding hoofs drew away. At two hundred yards distance, the Sioux grouped around Stone Heart.

Yells of triumph rose from their ranks as the excited warriors recited their individual *coups* counted in the charge. Instantly Pete shouted to his men to mount, and they began a thundering race toward the distant gap. No one but Kicking Elk stood in their way.

Bullets whined off stones on the ground around the defiant war leader's feet, cracked frighteningly close to his ears, and tore feathers from his tied-up warbonnet train. Calmly he stood his ground, Winchester held slackly at his waist. At fifty yards, with a veritable hailstorm of lead converging on him, Kicking Elk fired the rifle.

His first slug knocked Donny Barker from the saddle. The second did in Donny's younger brother, Mel. Still the courageous war chief did not flinch from his appointed spot. A slug bit into Kicking Elk's side an inch above his hip bone. His eyes narrowed slightly as he mentally inventoried and discovered it to be a shallow flesh wound. Again he sighted the Winchester.

A .44-40 bullet from the rifle sped on a collision course with Pete Miller's chest. Luckily for him, his mount slammed a foot painfully into a hidden stone and swayed to the left. Hot agony exploded along the outside of Pete's right arm as the projectile gouged a deep trough in his deltoid muscle. He instantly dropped his carbine.

Fighting the pain, Pete drew his Colt revolver and shifted it to his left hand. Not so competent a shot from that side, he tried to sight on Kicking Elk. But before he could, bright flowers of pain hurtled forward through his brain from the back of his head, and darkness swept over the gang leader.

The Sioux had caught up.

Stone Heart completed the follow-through with his warclub as Pete Miller slid from his saddle. The back of the outlaw's head had caved in, and a wet, red smear soaked his matted hair. Ahead of the trustworthy lieutenant, his courageous leader took aim on another of the treacherous whites.

Kicking Elk's .44-40 bullet smashed its way through the leather and wood pommel of a fancy Texas roping saddle. With it came a spray of slivers and ragged cowhide. They entered the gaping wound in Barry Howard's groin directly in concert with the slug. Instant inferno erupted in the young bandit's lower abdomen as the metal blob removed the head of his small, malformed penis and slivers of wood shredded the flesh of his scrotum.

Weakened, he sagged in the saddle as his horse bore him past the staked-out Sioux. His pain-fogged mind dimly recorded an incident that it discounted as hallucination. Instead of a final, killing round, the fierce-looking war chief reached out with dreamlike slowness and touched Barry with the hot barrel of his Winchester.

A second later, Barry galloped past. He twisted his head, uncertain and curious, to see what would happen next. Kicking Elk nodded and gave a cheery wave to his friend and second-in-command. Stone Heart closed on the mortally wounded outlaw.

Their movements could have been under water, Barry Howard thought as he watched the paint-daubed Sans Arc warrior raise his warclub and his own sluggish attempt to jerk his body out of harm's way. Slowly, ever so slowly it seemed, the small, egg-shaped stone began to descend. Another of those creeping seconds and he could get away safely, Barry thought. Then time returned to normal.

With a vicious swish, the warclub came down on its target, and its long, flexible handle added its delivery of energy to the swing. The oblong rock buried itself to the haft in Barry Howard's forehead. He made not a sound as he fell from his galloping beast. So tightly stuck in Barry's skull that it could not come free, the warclub pulled Stone Heart from his pony's back.

He landed in the dust beside his victim. Around and beyond him, the battle raged.

One by one the outlaws fell to arrow, bullet or lance. Two Ravens, of the Teton band, closed in on the last white man, only to get a bullet in his gut. With an angry howl, Gets-up-late raced in on the hardcase's blind side and drove his lance in between two ribs. A powerfully built man, Gets-up-late continued to force the shaft through his victim until it exited on the far side, dragging along bits of lung tissue, scraps of skin, and a piece of severed artery. A second later, only the victorious whoops of the Sioux could be heard outside the entrance to the gap.

Eli Holten couldn't believe his good fortune. He had taken a stroll down past the magazine building, a practice he had established early on. This time, he found not a soul outside or lounging in the interior. Pleased with this opportunity, he hurried inside.

One large, intimidating Whitworth gun sat on the floor, rigged for quick movement into position. Off near the concave arc of the brick wall, he saw a wooden square cut into the floor. It had a rope handle to pull it up and had been assembled with pegs instead of nails. The powder magazine. The scout made a quick check to insure he was indeed alone, then returned to the opening of the underground vault. Cautiously he raised it.

A rectangular box of heavy burlap prevented him from seeing down into the bowels of the earth. A spark shield, his mind supplied. He placed his boot carefully on the first tread and tested it to insure it would not squeak. Then he put his full weight on that leg and started, with equal caution, down into the magazine.

The musty scent of bulk black powder rose to tingle his nostrils. He dared not light a match. After a slow descent, he felt flagstones beneath the soles of his boots. By feel he began to examine the contents of the cellar room.

Long cases that must contain projectiles for the Whitworth guns he found stacked to the right of the stair. Directly ahead, round metal containers were revealed by his light touch. Twenty-five-pound cans of powder, he speculated. A short move to the left revealed a stack of silk bags, to be filled for propelling the slim shells. Also stacks of cartridge boxes and bales of cleaning waste. Eli's quick mind began to play, if only he could find a way to touch this off once the cavalry returned. Satisfied, he started up the steps.

His sudden return to daylight blinded him momentarily, so that his other senses warned of someone nearby before he could see. He dropped into a crouch and went for his gun before a familiar voice cried out in a hushed whisper.

"Eli! It's me. Marilee. You must hurry."

"What is it?" Eli's vision gradually cleared. "You look like someone's struck you."

"It's father. He's found out that you are a scout for the Army, and that the preacher is Amy Smith's husband. He's sent men to find you and lock you away until tomorrow. You'll be shot. You'll have to escape from here somehow."

"My horse. I have to get him from the livery."

"I've already done that. He's waiting outside."

"Good for you." Holten started for the tall, open doors to the magazine.

Outside, the street remained empty. He hurried to Sonny's side, swung into the saddle, and looked back at Marilee. "I'll be back. Do what you can to help Zeke. And look after Amy for us both. Help her and the others girls in whatever they plan."

"Oh, Eli, I'll simply die if anything happens to you."

"It won't. Not if I get away from here unseen."

Holten put spurs to his big Morgan and started off down the street at a lope. He made a block before an alarm sang out.

"There he goes!"

"Get him!"

"Open fire, damnit!"

"Mr. Yardley, make signals to the other gun, if you please," Captain Weatherby commanded from the balcony of the nearest bordello. "Tell them to open fire on the rider leaving town right now."

Men rushed toward the magazine in a desperate attempt to obtain their stored weapons. The first two wrestled with the stubborn locks while Eli Holten galloped closer to the edge of town. Meanwhile the dark balls of signal flags soared up the halyard and burst into colorful communication. Captain Weatherby continued to fume and pace the balcony. Two rifles cracked from the front doorway of the magazine. Then a third joined in.

Bullets whined past the scout as he spurred Sonny to greater effort. Suddenly, off to his right, a dull thud and boom sounded. Like lazy, summertime thunder, a large projectile crackled through the air and over his head. It struck some five hundred yards beyond with a ferocious explosion. Reflexively, Holten hunkered lower on his horse's neck and tried to urge more speed.

Another whump and billow of powder showed to him the hidden location of the Whitworth gun. Like its predecessor, the shell ripped air over his head and burst a good hundred yards beyond. At that rate, the gunners would have his range in no time. Thinking fast, Eli changed direction and raced toward the ugly excavations made by the bursting case shot. Ominously, the Whitworth fired again.

This time the charge went off short of him by a good three hundred yards. His ruse had worked! Sonny's churning legs had begun to widen the distance by even more. A fourth round also fell short, and Holten changed direction once more, headed directly for the yawning welcome of the narrow gap. A fifth projectile landed in line with him and three hundred yards to the rear. Desperately, Holten veered once more to throw the gunners off.

Again it worked, and the blast came muffled by even greater distance. Only three hundred yards separated him from the watercut canyon.

The next round shrieked over his head and burst high up on the wall of the cut. Two more followed while he closed the distance. They had that range registered, Eli thought with sinking hope. Then he began to count as he slowed Sonny's pell-mell flight.

Another shell burst ahead of him, and he counted again.

Abruptly, Holten reined in and waited while the thin, needle-pointed missile rippled the air above him. Instantly he jumped Sonny into a gallop.

"Three . . . four . . . five . . . six . . . seven . . ." Holten counted aloud, his lips peeled back in a scream of fatalistic determination. "Eleven . . . twelve . . ."

BAROOM! Sound from the firing of the Whitworth reached Eli as he lashed at Sonny's flanks with his reins. He had less than a second.

The cannon projectile screamed over his head and burst a hundred yards ahead.

"One . . . two . . . three . . . four . . ." the scout began counting again.

Sonny flashed past the ugly craters created by the shelling. Dark shade loomed ahead. Another fifty yards. Twenty. Ten . . . five . . . two. . . .

Earth ripped up behind him in great gouts. The force of the blast was nearly overwhelming. Sonny staggered, and the scout's ears rang with a special agony. His courageous stallion regained his footing and surged without further urging into the gap.

For the next three minutes, projectiles continued to fall, only blindly, bursting to the sides or behind Holten's position. The distance widened. New hope burned brightly in Eli's breast. Around another curve, and he would be out of range. Sonny made it easily. Holten cast an anxious glance behind to check for pursuit. He saw none and turned back as Sonny rounded the sweeping bow in the creek bank. Instantly, he pulled Sonny to a halt.

Struggling to keep his face calm, the scout looked directly into the eyes of Kicking Elk.

Chapter 17

Speechless fury burned to a fine white ash in Captain Weatherby's breast. The gun crew had behaved like a fumbling mob of helpless amateurs. Nine shots fired, and none of them had hit. What a waste of ammunition! Worse, the scout had gotten away, and he knew the position of the other gun.

"Mr. Yardley, assemble a relief and send them out to that gun. I want to see those men who did the firing as soon as they come back. Where is my daughter? What are you men standing around gaping at? Return those firearms to the magazine. Make haste, now."

In a flurry of arms and legs, the denizens of Breakneck Gap set about their tasks. Ten minutes later, while Weatherby descended the stairs to come out and take to task the members of the gun crew who had failed to prevent Eli Holten's escape, a rider pounded into town. He skidded to a stop at sight of the Captain and hurried in his direction.

"Somethin' awful, Cap'n."

"Later, my good man. First I must deal with these miscreants."

Imperiously, Weatherby stalked to a position in front of the errant gunners. "You men have disgraced yourselves and your captain irreparably. You not only missed your target and let him make fools of you all, but wasted precious ammunition for which there is not a current resupply. For the time being, you shall be confined to quarters, your daily grog ration suspended until further notice, and no social contact allowed with the inmates of our pleasure barges. I shall decide at an officers' conference if there are to be any floggings passed out. Boatswain, dismiss these men and put a guard on their quarters."

"Aye-aye, sir."

"Now, captain. This is awful news," the rider interrupted.

"What is it, man?" Weatherby snapped impatiently.

"You ever hear of the Pete Miller gang?"

"Certainly. Who has not? What does that have to do with Holten's escaping?"

"Nothing. Only—well, they was on their way here. I spotted 'em out on the slope beyond the gap. Got jumped by Injuns. Whole bunch of Sioux."

"And?" the Captain prompted.

"Kilt to the last man. Nothin' left worth buryin', either. Scalped, throats cut, tongues cut out, bellies opened. Gawdawful tormentin' of the wounded. I stayed as long as I could, then hightailed it here. Damned near got myself blowed up by the big gun. Who was that feller they were shootin' at? Looked like the deacon to me."

"It was. Only he's no deacon. That was Eli Holten, the scout for the Twelfth Cavalry," Weatherby informed him. "You were keeping watch in the gap?"

"Aye. Until I heard the Sioux."

"So," the Captain speculated. "If you were away from

your post, Holten had the opportunity to get cleanly away."

"Not for far he didn't. I never seen but his back as he rode into the gap. I done pulled my horse down and hid out while the shells whistled over. But if he got through the canyon without a shell blowin' him to bits, the Sioux got him."

"Hummm. A worthwhile thought, perhaps. Whatever the case, the savages won't stay long. They can't feed themselves if they tarry much in any place. We will have to send a party out to recover the corpses. See to it, Mr. Yardley."

"Aye-aye, sir."

With the disruption of their plan, Amy set to reorganizing the bevy of prostitutes in the three bordellos. One five-man crew of the Whitworths had been confined to quarters, which would make their job more difficult. A means would have to be devised of dealing with them. She made her way from one establishment to the next, talking, encouraging, giving out assignments.

"You three will be responsible for passing out rifles to each of the girls who can shoot. Once we seize the magazine, we will provide a diversion so that the cavalry can take the town easily."

"With those gunners in there, how do we go about that?" Sylvia inquired.

"You would ask that. I'll think of something. When I do, you'll be the first to know. When we first get in, someone will have to climb to the roof and take care of the two men there."

"I'm afraid of heights," Nadine protested.

"Me, too," Lenore agreed.

"You'll have to get over that. Once we have some form

184

of weapon, it will take two of us girls to finish off those sentries."

"When is this going to happen? There isn't much time before they—well, I heard that boatswain fellow say the Captain wants to shoot Reverend Zeke at sundown tomorrow."

"I'm working on that. We have a new ally. The Captain's daughter, Marilee. She's to try to stall that off until the cavalry arrives."

Reverend Ezekiel Smith hugged himself and paced the short space in front of the stored ice. How he wished for a pair of gloves and a thick, woolen muffler.

"I'm c- c- cold," little Geoffrey Tandy chattered.

"Come here, then," Ezekiel offered.

He opened his coat and clasped the boy close to his chest. Strangely, their combined heat seemed to ease his own chills. Geoffrey snuggled close, his own small arms wrapped around Ezekiel's middle. They huddled thus for half an hour. Then the bolt on the outside scraped, and the door swung open.

"Ain't that sweet, mates?" a Cockney voice cooed. "The Reverend's found himself a reg'lar pouge." Chuckles went among those who had been long to sea.

"You are an abomination," Ezekiel snarled. " We're both freezing in here. What did you come for? To gloat?"

"Oh, that. The Captain's compliments, and he wants to see you in his quarters. Just you, mind," the Cockney growled at Ezekiel.

"What about the lad? He'd catch his death in here."

"No matter. Here or on the yardarm tomorrow morning. What the hell difference does it make, rev'ren'?"

"Animals. Lead on, then. And be quick about it."

Five minutes later, Ezekiel Smith stood before Capt. William Weatherby's desk. So far he had not been enlightened as to the cause of the summons. Weatherby studied him coldly a moment, sipped from a glass of sherry, and pursed his lips.

"You may be a sneak and a blackguard, Reverend Piker, or Smith, as the case may be. But you are also a man of perception. You are learned and an advocate of a worthy calling. As such, you have pointed out something to me, a condition I had failed to make provision for." Weatherby paused and crossed to a large cherrywood sideboard with a tall, beveled-glass mirror. There he poured more sherry.

"The lad, Geoffrey Tandy, needs a barrister. An advocate, as it is called in the Royal Navy. I propose to make you his counsel."

"I'm not a lawyer," Ezekiel protested. "I am a minister of God."

"Even so. Would you not argue man's case before the Devil? Or before the throne of God? Well then, a mortal court should not intimidate you. You can do your best for the boy."

"He's not guilty of rape, you know," Ezekiel eyed Weatherby directly.

"Elizabeth says different."

"The Brewster girl is a vicious, spiteful, scheming little wretch. She is so full of the poison of self-righteousness that she has no room for the milk of human kindness nor the least dram of decency. I strongly suspect that she revealed their cozy little arrangement only because she suddenly grew fearful of becoming pregnant.

186

It's a shame the boy didn't teach her something about oral sex."

A sharp bark of laughter came from the captain. "For a preacher, you constantly amaze me."

"I was only stating the obvious."

"And most eloquently. You see? That is why I want to prevail upon you to act as the boy's advocate." Weatherby poured another crystal glass of sherry and offered it to Ezekiel. "I might add that whatever you do for Geoffrey will be considered in mitigation of your own crime."

"You, too, can be most eloquent, Captain. I, ah, accept."

"Excellent. The tribunal will sit promptly at nine tomorrow morning, following breakfast. And, ah, Reverend, give it your best. I'm, ah, fond of the boy, you see. Wouldn't want to send him to the gallows without every possible consideration."

"*Onś imaya!* I am Tall Bear of the *Oglalahca*," Eli Holten barked in Lakota.

"You are recognized, Tall Bear, without need to demand it," Kicking Elk replied.

They had sat for a long, frozen moment, neither moving a muscle or breaking their solid concentration. It counted greatly in the matter of face that the scout had seized the initiative in the conversation.

" *Hiyu wo*," the Sans Arc war chief demanded. Holten rode forward. "Among the *Itazipicola*, it is said that Tall Bear is *hmunga*. I do not dread your mystery. You are a changeling. A white man turned into red. Sometimes this works, other times . . ." Kicking Elk made an eloquent shrug.

"You say that Tall Bear is not *Odakotah*?"

"You, too, have now said it."

"I *am* a true Dakota. I do not make war on men who want peace. I do not murder women and children for no cause. It is you who seek to turn the prairie into a sea of fire and blood. It is you who are not *Odakotah*!"

"You were in the village of the evil whites," Kicking Elk challenged.

"Yes. To learn their weaknesses and strengths. I ride to the soldiers, who wait at Eagle Pass. Then we'll attack these men and drive them out."

"Your words are welcome. Why is it I don't believe you?"

"You must."

"Do you go to bring the pony-soliders against Kicking Elk and those who have joined him?"

"No."

"Still, I cannot let you go."

Holten's quandary sat heavily on his shoulders. He figured it would take two days to reach Eagle Pass. By then, the regiment should be formed and waiting there for his information. Then another harrowing ride back. That was a long time to keep Ezekiel from being killed. Any time wasted on distractions and unessentials was more than he could afford. Yet from the evidence he could see of mutilated corpses behind Kicking Elk, the war chief had indeed become someone formidable to resist.

"Kicking Elk, the Army truly wants to clear out Breakneck Gap every bit as badly as the Sioux. The soldiers are two days' ride from here. If your men are painted for war, why not join hands with your white warrior brothers, and together we can destroy the ones we want away from here?"

"You . . . mean . . . fight *beside* the pony-soldiers?"

Holten found Kicking Elk's dilemma grimly amusing. What would Frank Corrington say?

The general wouldn't have to like it — only authorize it. Right at that point, eliminating Breakneck Gap counted higher than diplomatic or military protocol. The two forces, fighting side by side, could exterminate the menace of Captain Weatherby and his small army of hardcases. Besides, his cynical side told him, the Sioux could be used as cannon fodder until the big guns could be neutralized.

"Consider it, Kicking Elk. Alone your force can only blockade this narrow passage and prevent anyone from entering or leaving. Alone, the Army can only do the same, until heavy guns that shoot a long way are brought up to shell the town. Both ways, time flies like the swift hawk. Together, we can overwhelm the defenders of the village and end it quickly. That is what you want, is it not? For the Sun Dance?"

"You would attend this sacred ritual?"

Eli didn't hesitate. "I would."

"You would participate in the *wiwanyag wacipi*, the sun gazing ceremony?"

"I . . . would." Memories of intense pain slowed the scout's reply.

As a boy of seventeen, he had entered the *Wambli* society of the Sun Dancers. It had entailed long hours of suffering, while dancing suspended from the Sun Dance pole by long rawhide cords, attached to plugs driven through the skin over his shoulder blades. He had chosen this particular lodge from worry over permanent damage to his eyes that occurred to more than a few

189

among those who followed the stricter and more demanding sun gazing ceremony.

The sun gazers had the plugs of wood inserted through the pectoral muscles of their chests and hung backward while they danced and sang and peered ceaselessly into the sun. It was this excruciating self-torture to which Kicking Elk had demanded he subject himself. If it took that sacrifice to prevent a general uprising, Holten steeled himself to accept. He could do it.

Kicking Elk urged his pony closer and placed a hand firmly on Holten's shoulder in the Sioux manner of masculine greeting. "I was mistaken. You are *Odakotah*. Come, we will announce this thing and sit in council to decide if our warriors fight together."

Chapter 18

"I find it unnecessary to have the child present or to have her testify," Capt. William C. Weatherby declared at five minutes past nine the next morning.

The trial of Geoffrey Tandy had been convened in a dusty, unoccupied storeroom behind the larger saloon. Boxes and barrels served for seating the spectators, and the tribunal sat behind a long, wide plank, held in place by two sawhorses. Cobwebs hung from the ceiling, and what light entered the room did so through grime-fogged windows. Reverend Ezekiel Smith and his client sat at a small, rickety three-legged table, obviously borrowed from one of the whorehouses. Dust motes hung in the air, disturbed by a handful of darting flies.

"Such an ordeal would prove entirely too trying on such a delicate personality as hers," he concluded.

"It is absolutely necessary that she be here *and* that she testify," the Reverend Ezekiel Smith insisted. "A man is entitled to face his accuser and to hear the evidence against him. That is guaranteed him in the Constitution."

"This is an Admiralty Court, and your Constitution has no jurisdiction."

"Like hell it is! This is Dakota Territory, the United States of America, and the protections of the Fourth, Fifth, Sixth, and Seventh Amendments apply to foreign nationals as well as to citizens. Bring Elizabeth Brewster in here, Captain, or this is nothing more than a mock trial."

Weatherby's eyes narrowed. "I cannot allow it."

"Have you any other witnesses? Anyone who can swear that they were present and observed this child allegedly being raped by the accused?"

"Of course not. If someone had been there, 'twould never have happened. 'Pon my soul, that's self-evident."

"Well, then. Without her testimony there is no charge and no case, and there can be no conviction," Ezekiel replied smugly, his brain fevered at such a taxing in a field of which he knew little or nothing.

"You are most persuasive, reverend. Boatswain, bring Elizabeth Brewster here."

Ten minutes passed before Elizabeth put in an appearance. To those present, it was not evident that she had spent part of that time rubbing her eyes with onion juice to make them red and weepy. She curtsied demurely to the three officers of the court and walked to the chair indicated.

"Now, then, dear Elizabeth," Captain Weatherby began soothingly. "It has unfortunately become necessary for us to ask you a number of questions. If you will raise your right hand, please, the boatswain, er, the clerk of this tribunal will swear you in."

"State your name."

"Elizabeth Brewster."

"Do you solemnly swear that the evidence you are about to give in the case now pending will be the truth, the whole truth, and nothing but the truth, so help you God?"

"I do."

"Take your seat."

Elizabeth complied and put on a hateful face, which she turned on a quailing Geoffrey Tandy.

"Now, Elizabeth," the imaginary Admiralty's Advocate, Mister Crenshaw, opened. "Would you state the nature of the charge you have made against Mister Tandy?"

"He—" she looked away and covered her eyes with a small lace square. "He—took advantage of me. Forced himself on me. Made me do . . . awful things."

"By that, you mean he took carnal knowledge of you?"

"Yes," came her tiny voice.

"Forcible intercourse, was it?"

"Yes."

"Over what duration did this take place?"

"Oh, it seemed forever. I hurt so badly, and there was," she blushed and glanced away again, "blood."

"I see. Well, then, did he say anything afterward?"

"Th-that if I told anyor. , he'd—he'd have my head off for it."

"Scandalous!" Crenshaw paced before the tribunal for a moment, then turned back to the witness. "What did you say or do that might have led the accused to believe such attentions would be welcomed?"

"Oh, nothing. I would never permit such—such licentious behavior."

"Think carefully. Not a word, a gesture, a longing look?"

"No. Nothing like that."

"No further questions. You may step down."

"Just a moment." Ezekiel rose. "I have a few."

The minister stalked from the small table allowed him and Geoffrey Tandy. "When asked the duration of this, ah, event, you said it seemed to go on forever. Is that because it happened more than once?"

Elizabeth paled slightly and tried to avoid Ezekiel's piercing eyes.

"Answer my question, child. Did you and Mister Tandy engage in intercourse more than one time?"

"Yes," came the whispered reply.

"Do speak up so the tribunal can hear you," Mr. Yardley demanded.

"I said, 'Yes.'"

"Thank you," Ezekiel responded. "Now, can you tell me approximately how many times? Was it twice? Three times? Four? A dozen?"

"Come now, advocate, you are intimidating this poor girl," Weatherby injected.

"Not at all, Captain. I seek only to discover the heinous nature of his crime."

"Answer, please," Weatherby commanded.

"It . . . well . . ." Elizabeth looked wildly around her at a sea of avid male faces. She felt dirty, exposed. "We, uh, did it three or four times."

"Over how long a period?"

"Each afternoon."

"*Each* afternoon? How many afternoons?"

"Four."

"Ah, yes. If you participated in intercourse with Geoffrey Tandy three or four times an afternoon for four afternoons, that makes it twelve to sixteen times all together. And you contend that these were all rape?" Elizabeth merely nodded, consumed with misery. Ezekiel went to the table where the tribunal sat. From it he lifted an inkwell and pen. These he took to the witness stand.

"Now, Elizabeth, I would like you to do something for me. Take this pen. Yes, that's right. Now, please put it in the inkwell."

Wearing a puzzled smile, Elizabeth did so with alacrity.

"That's very good. Now, take it again. If you would be so kind, put it back in the inkwell once more." When she tried, he moved the onyx container slightly. The pen missed. "Try again."

This time he moved the inkstand more violently away.

"I can't do it when you move around like that."

"Precisely. Thank you, Elizabeth." Ezekiel returned the implements to the table.

"Captain, gentlemen of the tribunal. Put yourselves in this girl's position. If you were raped, would you not want justice? Of course you would. That's why she is here today. If you had been raped twice, wouldn't you normally seek some means of protection from a repeat of the nasty experience? Of course you would. Had the unspeakable been attempted a third time, wouldn't you have put up some sort of struggle?

"But this girl contends that she was *forced* into this terrible situation on no less than twelve occasions, over a period of four days. And it could be fourteen, fifteen or sixteen. She's not certain of the actual number of times. And we are asked to believe that all of these abominable violations of her virtue occurred with no complaint — until now. With no request for a guard on her door — until now." Ezekiel shrugged and made long, deliberate eye contact with each of the three judges.

"Somehow, I find that rather hard to believe. Particularly after that movingly graphic demonstration of the difficulty of placing a rigid object in a wiggling hole. Yet she didn't say anything about resisting. Surely by the second afternoon when he came to you, you must have realized that keeping quiet was not going to make it all go away. Yet still you did not resist. Why was that?" Before Elizabeth could answer, Ezekiel went off on another tack.

"You said or did nothing to encourage him?"

Relieved to get off the subject, Elizabeth nodded energetically. "Oh, I'd never do a thing like that."

"What about . . ." Ezekiel rummaged in a vest pocket and produced a scrap of paper. "This? 'I long to have the tender touch of your hand upon my cheek, thrill to the closeness of your manly body. Come alone to my room this afternoon. Be discreet. I can promise you a garden of delicious treats.' It's signed, 'Passionately yours, Elizabeth.' To whom did you address that?"

"Why —" Elizabeth's eyes widened, and her pallor grew lighter. "It didn't say that. Those aren't the words. I — I wrote him to say I wanted him in my —"

"In . . . your . . . bed?" Ezekiel drawled out. "And you asked him first, isn't that right?"

"No . . . yes . . . I don't know."

"You wanted it mighty bad, didn't you? It felt good, what he did to you. You liked having that object slide in and out, in and out. It tingled and made you happy, didn't it?"

"No! No! No!" Elizabeth shrieked.

"Oh, but I say it did. Why else would you let him do that to you sixteen times?"

"Ooooh! *I hate you! I hate every one of you dirty, lusting men!*

196

Yes. Yes, it felt wonderful. He was shy. Ignorant of what to do, so I suggested he go and learn. After that—ooooh, I hate you for making me tell this."

"But it is the truth, isn't it, Elizabeth?"

"Yes. Yes, damn you."

"The defense moves for a dismissal at this time," Ezekiel said quietly.

The three judges conferred quietly for a brief few seconds. "The case against Midshipman Tandy is dismissed," Captain Weatherby declared in ringing tones.

For two days and two nights, drums beat a low, slow rhythm in Kicking Elk's camp. Smoke-talk signals had been sent, so that the troopers approaching Eagle Pass from Fort Rawlins knew of the changed situation. As requested by Eli Holten, a light, fast detachment would be sent ahead under command of Lieutenant Holland. Sioux guides would be posted along the route to direct them to the camp. When the camp crier at last brought news of their approach, the drums stopped.

"I'm glad to hear that," Eli admitted to Kicking Elk.

"You thought they might not come?"

"I was worried they couldn't get here in the time I set."

"Now we fight?"

"Yes, Kicking Elk. Now we will have a fight like none the world has seen before."

"A big fight?"

"I was thinking more of who is going to be on whose side."

The scout's words were echoed by Sergeant Liam McInnes an hour later, when the reinforced detachment of troopers rode into the Sioux camp. "Sure an' Mr. Holten ain't expectin' us to be fightin' alongside these heathens, is he?"

"It looks that way, Sergeant," Lieutenant Holland responded, his nose wrinkling distastefully at the overpowering odor of rancid bear grease. "I was perfectly willing to accept that your Mr. Holten is considered unorthodox. This, however, is stretching regulations to the utmost. Why, these savages aren't even supposed to be armed with any weapons capable of use in warfare. Yet, here we ride into a camp simply bristling with rifles, carbines, and revolvers, some of them more modern and efficient than what we carry. I tell you, I don't like it, sergeant. Not one little bit."

"Beggin' yer pardon, sir. But there be Mr. Holten with that tall war chief. My bet is it's Kicking Elk himself. We should be makin' ourselves known to them."

"Let the savages come to us, sergeant," Holland replied coldly.

McInnes scowled off to one side. He cleared his throat suggestively before making reply. "Sure an' that would be the way of it, were they to come to us. It appears as how it's us comin' to them. Such little things is important out here. To the savages, sir, if not to us."

Holland sniffed in disdain. "Very well, sergeant. Halt the troops and we'll advance to where Holten and that hostile are waiting."

"He ain't a hostile, long as he's fightin' on our side, sir. I don't wish to impose, but they're touchy devils. The least slight and we could all wind up with our throats slit."

"Isn't that a little overdramatic, Sergeant McInnes?"

"Oh, no, sir. Beggin' yer pardon', sir, but that's the why of the Sioux bein' called the Cutthroat Tribe by their enemies. Alive or dead, they slice open the throats

198

of their victims."

"Ghastly."

"Sure an' it's barbaric, it is. Onliest thing is, we have to live — or die — with it."

When the introductions had been made, a brief strategy conference followed.

"Colonel Dobbs is bringing up the rest of the regiment, along with artillery," Holland informed Eli and Kicking Elk. When this had been translated for the Sioux, he went on.

"We are to conduct probing operations until they are in place for a concentrated engagement."

"Probing, hell," Eli snapped. "If we give them enough time, they'll find a new place to hide that one Whitworth gun. Then it'll be guesswork, with a lot of men getting killed until it's located. Besides, Amy Smith and some sixteen white women from Eagle Pass are captive in Breakneck Gap. The Reverend Ezekiel Smith is a prisoner there, too. It could be that Weatherby might decide to eliminate his hostages to prevent witnesses against him. I for one want Amy and the other girls out safe as quickly as possible. We have enough men, lieutenant. Between your troops and the Sioux."

"I wouldn't concern myself overly with a flock of soiled doves, Mr. Holten."

Eli found his fury rising at an alarming rate. His flinty gray eyes narrowed and hardened into shards of lethal stone, piercing the inexperienced young officer's flesh. "You are a complete son of a bitch, aren't you, Holland."

"That's insubordination, Scout. Watch yourself, or I'll have you placed under open arrest."

Holten had to laugh. "Here? In this camp? How do

you propose to go about taking me into custody, lieutenant? I'll say what I please, so long as the truth is behind it. We must get those women free, and Reverend Zeke, too."

"He's right, Lieutenant," McInnes urged. "To these people, he's Tall Bear of the Oglala. One word an' sure, you'd be dead meat. This is a right friendly discussion for savages. But, faith, what do you think those young bucks behind us are doin'? They ain't whittlin' stick dogs fer their kids."

"You mean, we're being watched?"

"Sure as there's saints in Heaven. Those braves back there are from the *akicita*. And from the same warrior society, by the marks they wear. Take a look at the ones on the other side of the council fire. See them stuffed blackbirds braided into their hair? The *Kangi Yuha*, or Raven-owners Society, if I'm not mistaken. They can make a pincushion of yer back before you can fart, let alone draw that Colt outta yer holster, lieutenant, sir."

"I'll say it again, lieutenant," Eli Holten delivered in a steely tone. "You call it whatever you want. It's a reconnaissance in force, or a probe of the enemy's flank, or any of a dozen cute little military terms. But we are going to hit Weatherby and his brigands and hit them hard. I showed you where the Whitworth was when I came out. The other one is inside the magazine."

"What good does that do us?"

"We have friends inside. Allies. The girls from Eagle Pass, Amy Smith and—another young woman. From them I have learned that all most of the captive Sioux girls want is to get a knife in their hands. When we attack, they will be turned loose, and those who can shoot will get rifles and other small arms. Amy will have des-

200

ignated someone to spike that other cannon. Without mutual support, the center one will get overrun easily. They can only fire in one direction at a time."

"You're assuming a hell of a lot, Mr. Holten."

"I got out, didn't I?"

"And I've been wondering about that. A bit too much on the miraculous side, don't you think?"

"Spit out what it is that's caught in your craw," the scout growled.

"It wouldn't be the first time some civilian working for the Army turned out to be in collusion with the enemy. You have an Indian name. You obviously command respect from these people. It isn't too farfetched to speculate that perhaps you, the outlaws in Breakneck Gap, and the Sioux are all working in collaboration against the Army and the settlers."

"You insufferable bastard!" Holten shouted as he came to his feet. "Do you want to know why the Sioux show me respect? Why they let you ride in here and keep your hair? Because I promised them that the Army was on their side in this affair. That you were coming here to help rid the Black Hills of that scum over in the valley."

"Whatever made them believe you? And what made you think you had the authority to decide such a thing?"

"Oh, I have the authority. Don't ever doubt me, mister." Eli nearly trembled from the suppressed rage that boiled up from deep within. "As to why they would believe me . . ."

Reluctantly the scout rose and slowly removed his shirt. Then he turned so that the long, vertical scars of his Sun Dance ordeal could be seen by the Lieutenant. Unseen by the soldiers, scalding tears of shame rose to fill Eli's eyes. He should never have been compelled to do this. Should never have shamed himself and his adopted people by a braggardly display for such an ignorant slug as Lieutenant Holland.

For his part, Holland examined the aged scars, and his eyes widened. His face paled as Eli explained their meaning.

"I was seventeen years old at the time. I am a member of the Eagle Society of the Sun Dance, thanks to these scars. Oh, I danced, all right. From sunup to sundown. I nearly didn't make it. I had to run and dash myself against the braided thongs that held me so that the skin would rip and I could claim my place with the *Wamblipi*." Holten struggled to master his emotions, conquered them and turned slowly to confront the awed young officer.

"An ordinary Indian does not lie. An initiate of the Sun Dance is said to be incapable of lying. At least when it comes to a matter of honor. So they trust me. Frank Corrington does, too. If I say we can attack and win, then by God we can."

Uncomfortably, Lieutenant Holland cleared his throat. "Wh-when do we move into position?"

"Tonight. After midnight. All loose gear removed or tied down. The men will walk the last mile and a half. Everyone should be in position to attack at sunup. All we can hope is that Amy and the girls will be ready in town."

Chapter 19

A few minutes before midnight, Amy Smith heard a soft, scratching knock on the door to her room. It could not be a late-calling customer, she knew, so she rose from the bed. Amy padded across the room on bare feet, wriggling into a thin wrapper. Quietly, she whispered through the panel.

"Who is it?"

"Let me in," came the reply. "It's urgent."

"Who are you?" Amy inquired, though she suspected from the accent.

"Marilee Weatherby. Now please open up."

Once inside, Marilee came right to the point. "I promised Eli to help. We have to get your husband out of the icehouse. We'll need him when the time comes."

"I'd sort of like to have him back, anyway," Amy told her drily.

"Of course. But that isn't what matters now. Father is fixing up something awful for him. We have to do it in a way nobody knows about for some while."

"Is there such a way?"

"If we had a distraction for the guards, yes."

"I can take care of that. How do we go about it?" Amy responded, her voice quavering with anxiety.

"There's a small access port on the top of the building. We'll have to lift out blocks and tunnel through the ice, but it can be done."

"Good. Let me make some arrangements, and we can get started."

Quickly, Amy dressed and left the room. She walked quietly down the hall to the room occupied by *Siyo*, the young Sioux girl who had so enthusiastically initiated little Geoffrey Tandy into the mysteries of love. A light scratch awakened the youngster, and she came to the door in the nude.

"Yes? What you want?"

"I have a little job for you. You wanted to help get even with the men who stole you?"

"Oh, yes. What must I do?"

Ten minutes later, the two men standing watch at the ice house stared in utter fascination as an apparent dream came to life and walked toward them. Flared hips swayed, narrow waist undulated, while a coppery-skinned beauty approached, entirely bare. Her pert, young breasts jutted upward from a thin chest, emphasizing the wiggle of her soft, rounded abdomen. In the dim light of the stars, both men could make out enough to understand that this was no apparition. When she reached their station, she extended both hands to squeeze rapidly rising organs.

"You want have fun?" *Siyo* asked in her broken English.

"Uh, sure. But we're on duty now."

"What mean du-ty?"

"Our job. Guards. Watch house here."

"No. More good we have fun." *Siyo* emphasized her demands with firm jerks on two swollen members.

"Yeah. Yeah. Let's do it, Harry. Hell, who's gonna know? We can take turns."

"I don't know, Jim. We could wind up gettin' flogged." The Sioux girl gave him an extra firm tug. "Aw, what the hell. I'm hornier than a three-peckered billygoat anyway."

"We go together, yes? One front, one back—trade off?"

"Jesus! I—I ain't never done it that way," Jim declared in mounting excitement. "That good, little gal?"

"Most good. You like. Hurry. Come me, this way."

Silently, the two sentries stole off into the dark shadows after the dimly seen form of the naked Sioux girl.

"Now's the time," Marilee announced. She leaned a rag-padded ladder against the rear of the ice house and began to climb. Amy came after. Once on top, they needed all their strength to swing back the thick, heavy hatch. Below sat a stack of ice blocks.

"Let's get to work," Amy urged. "We set them to the side, right?"

"It's the best we can do," Marilee observed.

The two women went to their task with a will. Ice blocks, ranging from thick to thin, began to pile up beside them on the roof. After a while, Amy slipped into the hole and began to hand out more to Marilee.

"I can't see a thing in here," Amy hissed as she delivered another cake of ice.

"Who's that?" came her husband's muffled voice from behind.

"It's me, Amy. We've come to get you out."

"Hurry. I'm stiff with cold."

A few more blocks and Ezekiel's anxious face appeared in the opening, dimly illuminated by starshine. Amy wanted to kiss him, but they had limited time. Faintly, from a distance, she could hear the giggles of the Indian girl and the grunting lust of the men she entertained.

"Quick, Zeke, climb up and slide in here." Amy backed to the open hatch.

Only seconds passed before her husband slithered through the frigid tunnel and stood up beside her. He sucked in a long, deep breath.

"Free air. It smells so good."

"We'll have to put the blocks back," Marilee suggested.

"Of course. It would be a sure giveaway," Ezekiel agreed.

With three of them, the job went quickly. At last, they stood at the head of the ladder.

"We gotta back," Harry's voice urged from the dark pool of shadow.

"Let her finish me off, first," Jim protested. "She's got more suction than a windmill pump."

"Down the ladder," Marilee commanded. "Hurry."

Once on the ground, the trio made it to Amy's room without incident. There, safe at least temporarily, Amy threw her arms around her husband and gave him a long, passionate kiss.

"Keep that up and we'll miss all the action outside," Ezekiel told her smugly after their embrace ended.

Eli Holten completed his sweep of the valley and returned to where the troopers of the Twelfth and the Sioux waited. He spoke with Kicking Elk and Lieutenant Holland in a low whisper.

"The gun is still where it was when I escaped. Five-man crew and a youngster to handle the signal flags. Kicking Elk, send warriors to kill them. They are to wait for the relief crew. Should be coming about sunup. When those men are taken out, have one of your braves give a prairie grouse call. That will be the signal to attack."

"It is good. My other braves will surround the village?"

"Yes. They go in first. Quiet killing, if possible," Eli emphasized. "When the first shots are fired, the cavalry will charge. We'll have one Whitworth gun out of action. That leaves one to worry about. A lot of warriors and soldiers will die if it isn't taken care of. But that's up to Zeke Smith and the girls in town."

"You trust a—a preacher to do a job like that?" Holland asked, incredulous.

"I trust Zeke Smith. He's equal to the job."

"My warriors will want to take scalps, gather trinkets from white village."

"Later. After the fighting is over. Until both of those Whitworths are silenced, we haven't time for anything like that," Eli told him.

"I still think a man of the cloth is a poor choice."

"Holland, Zeke Smith is one of the best shots in the Territory. I've seen him kill three men in a matter of seconds. The truth of the matter is, I'd rather have him beside me right now than you. I've never seen you fight enough to know if you're any good."

Holland swallowed his anger. "Let's get on with it, the horses are becoming nervous."

"Three hours to daylight. Everyone in place within the next two," Eli commanded.

Hampered by the stygian blackness that followed false dawn, the sentries atop the magazine did not see the approach of a figure dressed like a gun crew member. Apparently a bit intoxicated, the gunner reeled unsteadily to the small judas gate in the big double doors of the brick building. There he hammered noisily in order to awaken one of the slumbering men inside. The racket at last attracted the sentries.

"You there, what the hell's the uproar about?"

"I wan' in," a slurred reply floated up to the roof.

"Dammit it all. You'll be on report for this. Lay off that, and I'll come down and let you in."

"Don' give a damn 'bout report. Lemme in."

"All right, all right."

A few long, tense seconds later, the judas swung open. "Now, get your ass in here befo—UNNNGH!"

One strangled cry of pain came from the guard's lips to end his sentence, as the sharp knife in Reverend Ezekiel Smith's hamlike hand ended his life. Swiftly the shadows came alive with movement. The liberated girls of the bordellos swarmed in through the small portal and went rapidly to work.

In pairs they descended upon the sleeping gunners. Deftly they flipped hammocks and trapped the occupants in nets of strong sisal fibre.

"Hey! What goes here?"

"Get yer hands offen me!"

"Jesus, yer spinnin' me supper up me gullet."

Startled exclamations came from many of the gunners, now firmly held in their own sleeping rigs. Knife blades flashed dimly in the light of a bull's eye lantern, and the men's protests changed to screams of pain and

208

208

horror as the women they had so long abused extracted bloody vengeance. The noise quickly attracted the other sentry, who ran down the stairs to meet a knife expertly thrown by Marilee Weatherby.

The sentry dropped his rifle and clutched his breast. His scream of agony ended when his body hit the stone floor. In less than two minutes, the butchery was over.

Three of the girls had become badly upset by their grisly activities and sought dark places around the circular wall to be sick. When his small force of women ended their excited whispers and their harsh breathing subsided, Reverend Smith stepped over by the Whitworth and slapped the breech with a firm, callused hand.

"It's time to get started, girls," he told them. "I want to see hands of those of you who can shoot a gun." He made a quick count. "Good. Now of you who can, how many think they can work a cannon?" Only two hands went up.

"All right. Then here's what we'll do. All of you who can handle a rifle, go with Amy and draw arms from the racks. Five of those remaining, come over here, and I'm going to teach you how to make this thing talk."

A rich pink confection, edged in stark white, banded the sawtooth ridge to the east when Eli's sensitive ear picked out the call of a prairie grouse.

"That's the signal. Kicking Elk, let them know you're coming," Eli announced.

"*Hu ihpeya wicayapo!*" the war chief cried.

"*Huka hey! Huka hey!*" his warriors chanted, their voices high and light with battle lust.

Screaming individual warcries, the Sioux braves kicked their ponies into action and charged toward the unprepared town.

Instantly a bell began to ring, and sleep-slurred voices shouted the alarm.

Slowly the town's defenses came to life. Apparently not everyone abided by Captain Weatherby's rules. Firearms barked from windows, and three Sans Arc warriors spun off of their mounts. More weapons opened up in town as a disciplined group assembled in the street and trotted to the far end to heave on the barricade wagons.

With painful sloth, the heavy freight carriages closed over the opening between buildings. At two other exits from Breakneck Gap the same scene repeated itself. Too late for the far one, as half a dozen braves streamed inside, and arrows twanged off buffalo gut strings to thunk meatily into quivering human flesh. Elsewhere, most of the white men rushed toward the magazine to retrieve their arms.

A bad mistake, they found as a grinning Reverend Ezekiel Smith swung open the doors. He directed his improvised gun crew to roll the Whitworth forward and personally slammed one of the brass balls on the inertial starter.

The breech swung wide.

"Load canister," Ezekiel commanded.

Girls assigned to the duty of powder monkeys ran forward with powder bags and shells. Quickly a projectile was rammed home, followed by a silk bag of powder. The breech slammed shut.

WHAM! The inertial starter did its work, and Ezekiel yanked the lanyard.

Confined partially inside the big brick building, the

blast seemed enormous. Beyond the muzzle, at pointblank range, men screamed horribly and fell to writhe in the dust.

"Give 'em another one!" the minister shouted gleefully.

Outside of town a dozen filth-encrusted buffalo hunters stroked the long barrels of their Sharps buffalo rifles and waited under orders of Mr. Yardley. Soon a group of five men in white duck trousers and blue polka-dot shirts arrived.

"All right, now, men. You know what you have to do. Get to that other cannon and put it in action. Your primary target is to stop that other gun. Kill anyone around it and hold the place until these damned savages have had enough and start running," the first officer of Weatherby's imaginary ship commanded.

"We'll pick off them Injun bastards for ya, Mr. Yardley. Don't you worry none."

Behind Yardley, the other Whitworth boomed ominously, and he frowned with agitation. "My picked men didn't fare so well. See that you do so, and right smartly."

"Aye-aye, sir," the buffalo hunters' spokesman responded sarcastically. "Right by the fucking Royal fucking Navy book, sir."

Howling like banshees, the scruffy hide hunters raced across the ground to the Whitworth emplacement. Their big fifty-calibre Sharps buffalo rifles roared into the growing light of dawn and two darker forms near the hidden gun spun and fell out of sight. Arrows slithered through the air all around, and one of the tough, ugly ravagers of the plains grunted in

211

pain and fell. His comrades streamed on past him, re-loading on the run.

Swiftly the other braves who had captured the gun position died at the hands of these deadly gleaners. At their signal the gun crew ran forward and directed the burly hunters to horse the weapon around to train on the town. Within three minutes of the time they left the shelter of the buildings, the first round roared out of the muzzle of the Whitworth.

Chapter 20

Startled by the explosion, Ezekiel Smith watched while the false front of the Stag and Hound saloon erupted in a cloud of splinters and metal shards.

"Looks like we have competition, ladies. Double loads for everyone. Bring out as much powder and shot as you can. Hurry, now."

With grunting, panting effort, the reverend and the women of his crew wheeled the Whitworth gun out into the street. All others loaded down with two projectiles and two bags of powder each. Another incoming round smashed into the flimsy outer wall of a bordello and hurtled inside before exploding. Moments later, flames flickered in all the shattered windows. Ezekiel Smith made some hasty calculations and yanked the lanyard.

In a flat arc, the projectile shrieked out of town and burst three hundred yards beyond the second Whitworth.

"Load her up and we'll try again," Ezekiel commanded gleefully as he adjusted the range.

Around him to both sides, rifles and shotguns set up a steady rattle of fire as the armed prostitutes opened up on residents attempting to rush the gun or get inside the magazine to their weapons. Another incoming shell growled its way overhead and burst high on the parapet of the magazine.

A shower of brick chips and red dust raced outward from the center of the blast. Ezekiel shook his head in exasperation.

"Damn," he cursed. "They've got everything ranged." Then his expression cleared and became cheerful.

Far in the distance he heard the crisp, clean notes of a bugle, sounding the charge.

"We're being invited to the party," Eli announced to Lieutenant Holland when he heard an increase in the rattle of gunfire from the town.

"Sergeant McInnes," Holland snapped.

"Yes, sir. Prepare to draw carbines. . . ." Muffled equipment scraped leather as the troopers grasped the stocks of their weapons and loosened them in the scabbards. "Draw . . . carbines."

Another prolonged hiss of metal over leather.

"Trumpeter," Lieutenant Holland commanded in a heavy voice. "Sound the charge."

The notes fairly tripped over each other as the trumpeter let loose a shout of music.

Troopers yelled fierce cries and fired their carbines as they thundered down on the town, where two buildings already blazed. One third of the troops, under command of Lieutenant Holland, swung to the left, headed for the recaptured Whitworth.

Trapped into a gun duel, the breech-loading cannon remained pointed at the town, in an attempt to silence its counterpart. Ahead, Holten could see the Sioux braves swarming through the streets, killing everyone who moved.

He had to get to Ezekiel and the others to insure that they did not fall victim to overzealous warriors. Another shell burst in town, and a portion of a saloon roof rose in the air. Then a projectile from the gun in town struck the tree tops above the hidden Whitworth, and a shower of limbs, leaves, and steel fragments rained down.

"One more and they'll have the range," Holten said aloud, though no one could hear him.

Then the troops pounded into town and the situation got busy.

"Down two," Ezekiel muttered to himself as he cranked the elevating screw. "Ready! Fire!"

The Whitworth bellowed. At such short range, barely a quarter second went by before the shell burst at the base of a tree trunk near the enemy gun.

Buffalo hunters shrieked and flopped spasmodically on the ground, sieved by shrapnel. Two of the gun crew went down.

"We'll try another case shot this time," Ezekiel told the powder monkeys.

Another blast and sudden bright flash in the trees. More men screamed and toppled to the ground.

"One more should do it," Ezekiel observed aloud.

The opposing gun lifted in the air as its barrel rang musically, struck by the speeding artillery shell. Slivers of steel and a payload of lead balls slashed at the surviving men. Two more died, and the position became indefensible.

Survivors among the buffalo hunters and the crew leaped up and started to run. Directly into the path of the oncoming cavalry.

One crusty old hand got off a shot. It nicked Lieutenant Holland in the left shoulder. Four hundred fifty grains of lead packed enough punch to unhorse the charging officer. Before he hit the ground, a fusillade ripped from the Springfield carbines of the troopers. Buffalo hunters and gunners littered the ground after the smoke cleared. Only the oldtimer remained, sitting astride the officer's chest, slashing at Holland's throat with a skinning knife. A trooper close to the gruesome deed released his hold on his carbine and let it swing on the securing lanyard as he turned his horse and bolted to the aid of his commander.

He arrived too late, as thick, twin streams of blood geysered into the air from Edward Holland's severed throat. In a rage, the soldier drew his sabre and swung it in a deadly accurate arc. It bit into flesh, and the grizzled buffalo hunter's head leaped from his neck to bound off across the gore-slicked grass. Ezekiel forced his gaze away from the scene of horror in order to issue more commands.

"Turn this piece around. We're going to take out the magazine."

"From this close?" Amy inquired, uncertain. She had seen the powder stored below ground.

"No. We'll back up a bit," her husband told her.

Precious minutes passed as they readjusted the powerful cannon. Then Ezekiel yanked the lanyard once more.

One round through the open doors caused the building to bulge outward and start to disintegrate. A fraction of a second later, the powder magazine let go.

The tremendous blast knocked everyone off their feet.

Right then the cavalry entered town.

Eli Holten had watched much of the attack through

216

field glasses. It made him aware that Weatherby ran the defenses from his suite in the largest brothel. He headed directly that way when he swung Sonny's head away from the terrific blast at the magazine. Windows shattered, and debris whistled past his head. In three fast bounds, Sonny reached his master's destination.

Holten swung out of the saddle and ran onto the porch of the big whorehouse. It remained the only building in town not blazing mightily. The scout kicked open the front door and dashed for the stairwell. From above, Eli could hear Captain Weatherby shouting desperate commands to his rapidly disintegrating defense.

Guided by the voice, Holten took the steps three at a time. In the hallway above, he oriented himself and headed for where the mad captain still ran his ship. Two henchmen waited for him.

A bullet cut through the scout's buckskin shirt and gouged a painful ribbon of flesh from along his ribs. It staggered him, and his first shot went wild. Holten worked the action of the Winchester and fired from the hip.

Hot lead punched a .44-40 sized hole in one gunhawk's belly. He reeled backward into his companion and then sagged to the floor. Before the second bodyguard could bring his sixgun into play, he looked down the black hole in the scout's rifle.

Flame erupted, masked in the following smoke. It was the last thing the Breakneck Gap gunman saw. Holten's slug smacked into his forehead, and he flipped backward against a wall.

Outside in the streets, the Indians, cavalry, and the ladies of the Thunder Saloon unleashed a veritable orgy of killing. Men who once considered Breakneck Gap a secure haven from the violence that filled most of their lives suddenly found themselves in a futile battle to save themselves from destruction. Wave after wave of blood-thirsty enemies seemed to rush at them. Several stared in shocked disbelief as Indians and cavalry fought side by side. Their incredulity quickly cost them their lives.

"Sure an' it's a hell of a way to fight a war," Liam McInnes shouted at a grinning Sioux warrior who stood beside the troop sergeant, wielding a warclub and toma-hawk. "Last time I seed ye, Spotted Pony, ye tried to stick an arrow in me."

"You want I do again?" the Sioux inquired in high spirits.

"Naw. Ye can be leavin' that to these rabble we're fightin'. Decorate a couple o' *their* chests with some shafts, and I'll be right pleased."

"Me do." Spotted Pony left off bashing in the head of a wounded hardcase to take up his bow. Swiftly he aimed and loosed a shaft that plunged deeply into the chest of Weatherby's second in command.

Mr. Yardley formed a silent "Oh" with blood-frothed lips and leaned back against a burning building front. He hardly felt the heat as he clawed at the arrow which had pierced his chest. Gurgling from one blood-filled lung, he grew more feeble with each attempt to remove the painful object. His eyes filmed, and he blinked to restore his vision.

It did him no good as a second shaft punched through his throat, and the broad, pounded steel point severed his spinal cord.

"Nice shootin'," McInnes observed.

A moment later, a fifty-calibre slug from a buffalo

rifle dashed the sergeant's brains against Spotted Pony's face and bare chest, and McInnes's promising career with the Army ended in a bloody puddle on the main street of Breakneck Gap.

From her vantage point near the Whitworth gun in the center of town, Rachel Johnson scribbled rapid, scrawled notes on a thick pad of paper while the carnage went on around her.

With lightning speed, the vengeful troops of the Twelfth Cavalry and courageous braves of the Sioux Nation descended on the town of Breakneck Gap. Blazing guns roared on all sides as this reporter stood by the mighty cannon which had been captured only moments earlier. Serving with the gun crew, your correspondent helped bring fire on the second of these infernal weapons, stationed some distance from town.

What delight we all felt when a well-aimed shot put the dastardly field piece out of commission. With renewed enthusiasm, we turned to giving support to the attacking forces of righteousness as they swarmed down on the community of desperadoes. How our hearts thrilled to the sound of pounding hoofbeats as painted warriors and blue-clad troopers rushed at the demoniacal defenders. At a suggestion from your reporter, the stalwart Reverend Ezekiel Smith trained our cannon on the powder magazine and blew it into fragments. Limited now in arms and ammunition, the bandit community nevertheless continued to put up a spirited defense. Many a brave man fell among the attackers as —"

"Look out!" Ezekiel shouted at Rachel.

She leaped to one side as a burning timber from one of the buildings fell past her shoulder. Sparks blistered her cheeks and singed her hair. To her sudden horror, she realized she had dropped her note pad and it now lay, being consumed by hungry flames, under the blaz-

219

ing wooden beam. All her work! Through tear-filled eyes she watched her prize-winning story literally go up in smoke. Then she recognized Eli Holten as he swung off his horse and entered the remaining bordello. Her heart raced, and her well-used cleft moistened.

Another familiar figure came into view and she nearly swooned with naked desire. Kicking Elk! Unbidden, she nearly ran to his side. Now her heart skipped a beat in every three at the sight of her Indian lover. Oh, how she had missed him. A bullet from the rifle of a buffalo hunter screamed past her head, and she dropped to the ground.

Eli Holten found the door standing ajar. Immediately cautious, he leaned his empty Winchester against the wall. He advanced silently and took a quick glance inside, his Remington revolver leading the way. Two men stood on the balcony. One Holten recognized as Captain Weatherby. The other was a leather-tough, burly buffalo hunter. The scout made a quick check of the rest of the room and entered in a rush.

He remained undetected as he made his way toward the open French doors.

"By gad, man. It looks as though everyone has turned against me," William Weatherby observed to the smelly hunter beside him.

"Not all of 'em. My boys is doin' their share."

"True, and I'm grateful. Only I'm afraid there's no hope. I must find my daughter, bring her to her senses, and escape this place. You'll act as our guide and protector, sir?"

"Right ye are — fer enough money."

"You'll have it. That I promise."

"You're not going anywhere," Eli Holten announced from the doorway to the balcony.

Both men turned.

Rattlesnake quick, the buffalo hunter got off a shot that slammed into the meaty portion of Eli's right shoulder.

The force of impact ripped the Remington from Holten's hand and spun him back into the room. He rammed into a low, stuffed chair and flipped backwards over it. Already the keen-eyed hunter had reloaded and bulled his way into the darkened room after his quarry. He stopped abruptly when he saw nothing of his prey.

"I gotta finish him off. I'd swear I only put it in his shoulder."

Eli Holten crouched behind the bulky furniture, his Bowie knife clutched tightly in his left hand. He used his keen senses of hearing and smell to track the odorous game slaughterer around the living room of the suite. Silently, he pivoted to keep himself ready. When the scruffy man showed himself, Holten leaped at him with all his strength.

The Bowie flashed through the air and opened a long gash across the buffalo hunter's belly. He dropped his Sharps and howled in agony.

With a quick, vicious backstroke, Eli brought the sharpened false edge across the bulky hunter's throat.

A thin red line appeared.

With a dreamlike quality, its lips spread wider and released a thin sheet of crimson.

Yawning wide now, the wound separated so that the severed cartilage of the man's larynx could be clearly be seen. An expression of astonishment washed over his face, to be replaced by the squinting, tortured visage of a person in excruciating pain. His mouth worked and his tongue protruded, as though seeking to escape the ravaging of his gullet. Splattered with a profusion of blood, the scout stepped away and turned to face Weatherby.

Eyes wide, lips writhing in speechless horror, the former sea captain raised both hands in mute appeal. His normally pale complexion whitened and took on a sickly greenish tinge as his legs went rubbery. As Holten advanced on him, a shot blasted from the doorway, and Weatherby collapsed.

Instantly the scout whirled and dropped low. To his amazement he saw Elizabeth Brewster standing on the threshold, a smoking revolver in her hand.

"He treated me mean," she stammered out. "Wouldn't punish that naughty boy for what he did to me. I showed him. Didn't I?"

Holten could only nod.

"Then, I thought I would never see home again," she explained, dredging up the painful memories of the past few days. "I—I let myself go. But now I'm free. Really free. Only I'm ruined. A soiled, used husk to be spurned by all decent folk. There's but one answer for me."

With a painful wrench, she turned the revolver on herself.

Eli Holten leaped across the room and grabbed the hot barrel of the Colt before the girl could cock the revolver again. He wrestled the weapon from her hand and tucked it in his belt. Elizabeth began to sob.

"It's all over now. You can go back to living the way you did," he told her. "No one need ever know what happened to you here."

"D-do you mean it?" Hope shined through the self-imposed degradation.

"Of course. Now, let's hurry," the scout added, sniffing the air in the hallway. "This place is on fire."

By the time he reached the streets with a docile and downcast Elizabeth, the destruction of Breakneck Gap was complete. Every building in town blazed, and the defenders had all died at the hands of the soldiers and their Indian allies. In the midst of the ruin, Eli located Amy Smith.

"Take care of Elizabeth for me, will you?" he asked.

"I will," she began reluctantly. "Only she did such wretched things."

"That's all part of a past best forgotten," the scout informed her. "Is everyone accounted for?"

"Yes. More or less. Sylvia was killed by one of Weatherby's men. I shot him myself. And there's someone who claims to be a newspaper correspondent over there hugging the daylights out of Kicking Elk. He don't seem to mind in the least."

Eli glanced across the blazing bordellos of Breakneck Gap to see Rachel Johnson in the arms of the brawny Sioux war chief. She's found something new, obviously. Eli shrugged. It was her choice, after all.

"So, after my notes were burned up," Rachel's voice drifted over to Eli's hearing, "I decided the only wise thing to do was forget the newspaper business and devote the rest of my life to making you happy."

"You good woman, *Anpagliwin*," Kicking Elk said through a smile of contented happiness as he gave her a new name.

"What does that mean?" Rachel inquired in her limited Lakota.

"Return-at-dawn Woman. We attack as sun come up.

You here to meet me. I am content."

Eli Holten shrugged. So what? There were lots of other women. Plenty for him. He silently wished the enamored pair happiness. Yes, lots more lovely ladies for him. Especially, he thought with quickening heart, this one.

Crying with joy, her face smeared and smudged with powder smoke, Marilee Weatherby dropped the rifle she carried and ran with open arms into the welcoming embrace of Eli Holten.

"Oh, Eli! Eli! Oh, I love you so!"

Where, the scout wondered, would this lead by the time winter set in?